BOOK TWO: THE AGE OF ICEMEN

PART ONE; AGE OF ICE

DESTINY WITH EVIL
BOOK TWO: THE AGE OF ICEMEN
PART ONE: THE AGE OF ICE

Written by:

Howard R. Vollmer

Illustrated by:

Howard R. Vollmer

Maps and Diagrams:

Howard R. Vollmer

DESTINY WITH EVIL

BOOK ONE: THE CALLING OF THE WAY

BOOK TWO: THE AGE OF ICEMEN
PART ONE: AGE OF ICE
PART TWO: COMING OF AGE

BOOK THREE: THE SHADOW OF EVIL
PART ONE: GROWTH OF A NATION
PART TWO: WHEN EVIL STRIKES
PART THREE: THE INTELLECTUAL STATE

BOOK FOUR: GOODNESS STRIKES BACK
PART ONE: DOMINION OF EVIL
PART TWO: PREPARATION OF THE FREEDOM FIGHTERS
PART THREE: FREEDOM RESTORED

This book is dedicated to all those who have curious minds and love to wonder in unknown worlds of forbidden space and time.

AuthorHouse™
1663 Liberty Drive
Bloomington, IN 47403
www.authorhouse.com
Phone: 1-800-839-8640

© 2013 by Howard R. Vollmer. All rights reserved.

No part of this book may be reproduced, stored in a retrieval system, or transmitted by any means without the written permission of the author.

Published by AuthorHouse   02/12/2013

ISBN: 978-1-4817-1726-7 (sc)
ISBN: 978-1-4817-1727-4 (e)

Library of Congress Control Number: 2013902915

Any people depicted in stock imagery provided by Thinkstock are models, and such images are being used for illustrative purposes only.
Certain stock imagery © Thinkstock.

This book is printed on acid-free paper.

Because of the dynamic nature of the Internet, any web addresses or links contained in this book may have changed since publication and may no longer be valid. The views expressed in this work are solely those of the author and do not necessarily reflect the views of the publisher, and the publisher hereby disclaims any responsibility for them.

TABLE OF CONTENTS

ILLUSTRATION INDEX	VII
FORWARD	IX
INTRODUCTION	X
PROLOGUE	XIII
CHAPTER 1: THE ANCIENT MAN AWAKES	15
CHAPTER 2: THE JOURNEY BEGINS	24
CHAPTER 3: THE HUNTER BECOMES THE HUNTED	34
CHAPTER 4: SOMEONE HIGHER MUST BE GUIDING THEM	42
CHAPTER 5: SKEPTICISM AND THE GOOD SURPRISE	48
CHAPTER 6: THE PLAN, NO ICE, & THE GREEN REWARD	58
CHAPTER 7: RONDEVOUS WITH DANGER	71
CHAPTER 8: THE COLONY SAVED & AWAITS THEIR HEROES	83
CHAPTER 9: THE HEROES WELCOME & A SON'S REPLY	89
CHAPTER 10: WARMTH, SWEAT, & THE RUBALANGERS	96
CHAPTER 11: THE LAND CLAIMS ITS OWN	106
CHAPTER 12: ATTACK FROM THE SKY & INJURIES ARE HEALED	121
HAPTER 13: A NEW BEGINNING AS THE JOURNEY ENDS	132
CHAPTER 14: NATURER'S FORCES & THE FRAGILE MAN	148
CHAPTER 15: GEO-MAGNETIC FORCES*SADNESS MIXED WITH JOY	159
APPENDIX A: NAMES & FACTS ABOUT PEOPLE	172
APPENDIX B: NAMES & FACTS ABOUT PLACES	182
APPENDIX C & D: FACTS ABOUT ANIMALS, BIRDS & THINGS	188

ILLUSTRATIONS & MAP INDEX

OHNIK	I
TROLLDAR	III
TROLLDAR	V
MAP OF THE COLONY'S JOURNEY	VIII
KIBLING	XII
TROLLDAR	XIV
AGE OF ICEMEN GREETING	23
KUPABIN	24
SWORDENFIN TUBRES	26
OHNIK CAVE WITH GLOWING BALL OF KNOWLEDGE	33
CLOSE UP OF JOURNEY BEGINNING	36 MAP
TUBRES GORGE	37 ILL
THE DEMON BEAST	41
KIBLING'S CAVE ART	47
KUBALLAR'S SURPRISE	57 ILL
TROLLDAR	70
BIBUTSAKUFASCORCHUM AND DAGGAR	79
DEATH OF BIBUTSAKUFASCORCHUM	82
HERO'S WELCOME	88
A SON'S MEMORIAL	94 ILL
CLOSE UP MAP OF CENTRAL JOURNEY	95 MAP
TUCKSAY NARROWS & THE RUBALANGERS	105
CAMPING AT BACSRIS CANYON	120
DANGER FROM THE SKY	122 ILL
CLOSE UP MAP OF FINAL JOURNEY	131 MAP
COMPTES & NAVITONA IN MOUNTAIN PRAYER	137 ILL
HUNTERS CATCH THEIR PREY	141 ILL
GOULA	142 ILL
BORGAMUTH	147 ILL
TROLLDAR'S RESCUE AT THE THREE CANYONS	150 ILL
KIBLING'S TRAPS & SNARES	157
THE FORCE FIELD KILLINGS	170
COMPTES	172
DOOMAGNON	181
ANIMALS AND BIRDS	188-191
CAVE OF THE GLOWING BALL OF KNOWLEDGE	192

MAP OF JOURNEY FROM FERIANDIMAL TO THE PROMISED LAND

FORWARD

There are many scientists that have paved the way to our understanding of those early years of Earth's beginning. We should be grateful to those many scientists in the fields of geology, archeology, anthropology, and astronomy who have labored, both in the field, and in the laboratories, to collect, organize, identify, and try to name those fragments of our past and those sightings through their telescopes. Earth scientists have solid substance to collect, analyze, and dissect. Even anthropologists and archeologists have a world of data in all the diggings throughout the world. But, all is not so concrete and established as some would have you believe. They too have argued and see-sawed their theories back and forth as new data comes in and the old is thrown out. The scientist also has many varied speculations of the missing parts to our puzzle of early times.

I thank them for this wealth of knowledge. As an artist, I have the liberty to study this information, digest it, turn it around, upside down, play games with it, and produce a work of my own imagination, one I hope will give hours of enjoyment and entertainment. The artist speculates on these ideas much differently than the analytical scientist. The scientists by their own training and nature are linear thinkers, that is, they use their time putting their data together for presentation and approval in a forward path, usually never looking from side to side. It is not in their interests to see the rest of the world with all its wonders. An artist, who is a peripheral thinker, see the world as 360° and all that is in it. The artist can make believe, expand on substances, theories, and on age old myths and tales. I thank the Good Lord that He has given us both the linear, analytical mind and the peripheral creative mind, for without both, the world would truly suffer.

INTRODUCTION

In the ice age, before men had time to sit and think, there were these men of survival. These men of survival were men of the North Camp, the land of Feriandimal. What was this special place where men dare to survive the ultimate diversities? It was a special place that nature set aside for human existence. A place in the frozen tundra where usually no one survives. It was different with these Icemen, for they had survived in caves thousands of years before the great tragedy that catapulted a large chunk of Earth into another dimension.

Our story begins with the ice men sound asleep in their cave. Then a tremendous explosion happened on Earth. A large asteroid hits Earth, causing such interruption of normal life, that the Earth's life forms would take thousands of years to recover. This was not the only catastrophe, for unknown to history, a gigantic eruption of forces caused a large part of the Earth to transcend into another dimension called Dimensia 4. It all started with a series of geo-magnetic forces colliding together and causing such a disruption that this large entity of matter, broke forth into space, and planted itself into another dimension. Most living creatures did not survive this catastrophic explosion, but those, either strong enough or sheltered in caves, were fortunate enough to survive. There were other creatures that also escaped. Some helped feed these brave men and others that will unfold in our story. Every creature, big and small, strong and weak, that survived, was ultimately mutated and transformed into new and different species.

Dimensia 4 existed for hundreds of thousands of years, ever evolving and changing into what was present when our story takes place. The men that evolved were even stronger and survived even more

INTRODUCTION (continued)

than men on Earth. These men were strong and resilient, not only to weather, but the strength and cunning of their predators. They fought off many large beasts and killed many of them for survival. They were, in fact, so extra ordinary, that Theasium took notice from high in his realm and sent his special wizards to come to their aid.

Not all was right with the Age of Icemen. These men were sheltered from the mainstream of the humanity in all the galaxies. Because of this, they were far behind other cultures of many planets. So Theasium not only sent his wizards to aid them but gave the wizards a challenge. He spoke to the High Council of Wizards saying, "My good and loyal Stewards, as you know, I gave you word that you are to help these strong resilient Age of Icemen advance and catch up to the rest of cultures in our great domain. They are pure and innocent, living in harmony with the laws of Nature and in conformity with the principles of the Highest Being of the Universe. But that is not enough, soon some other alien outsider will stumble upon them and they will be victims of their own innocence. I therefore command you to find some way to upgrade and bring these people into a cultural level where they will be equals if not better. It is up to you how you are to do this, but I give you two millenniums to carry this out." With those words, Theasium left the wizards to carry out their mission.

The wizards spent much time planning and developing a strategy to help these people. Finally after many sessions and debate, Trolldar came up with the solution. Place the Glowing Ball of Knowledge in a cave and lead them to it as necessary. This will shorten the time of advancement into the modern world by eons.

INTRODUCTION (continued)

nominated Do-o-magnicent to carry out the task and Trolldar would watch their movement and growth as a people. And so it was that Do-o-magnicent planted the Glowing Ball of Knowledge and alerted the Age of Icemen's leader to where it was and Trolldar moved in to watch their ever movement.

PROLOGUE

In the first book, Coming Of the Way, Trolldar enlisted the Mountain Trail Alliance to help him stop the evil forces from over running Dimensia 4. He tricked the Alliance into following him into another dimension, namely, Dimensia 4. He did this by attaching himself to the dreams of an artist, named Hedley Hoffman, who was clairvoyant and inadvertently got Trolldar's image in his mind and became obsessive in his pursuit to carve his head as a part of his walking cane.

Trolldar takes the Alliance through Mystic 3 passage, into Dimensia 4. Here, along with the key leader from Etudadorma, to acquaint them of the seriousness of what the evil forces were doing, led by Doomagnon and his henchman, Baulstar.

After the tour and signing of the Pledge of the Freedom fighters' Oath, Trolldar takes them back to Earth, where he promises them in their dreams and spare moments alone, he will fill their minds with the history and updates of Dimensia 4.

Our story begins with Trolldar's history lesson number one. His lesson starts with the story of the Ancient Ones, who discover a glowing ball and are propelled into a higher state of knowledge. These northern people of Feriandimal, are called the Age of Icemen. This glowing ball possesses their mind and they are driven to travel to the Middle Kingdom which later, they call the Promised Land. It is here that they are reacquainted with a second glowing ball, that they now call, the Glowing Ball of Knowledge. This ball is planted by the High Order of Wizards, by order of Theasium (see Introduction in book one, Coming of the Way).

The contact of this glowing ball, a second time,

PROLOGUE (continued)

thrusts them forward into an advanced state of cultural growth in religion, government, housing, arts, scientific and mathematical insights, and domestication and agriculture. As, with many, great societies, this accelerated social and economic growth led some to become greedy, envious, and hungry for power.

Doomagnon, who formally was called Do-o-magnicent for his supreme leadership in the High Council of Wizards, also falls victim to greed, power, and corruption. He then convincing Baulstar into becoming an evil dictator. Now, Baulstar in his new role, sees himself as the emperor of all Dimensia 4. His destiny is to capture and enslave all the people, by using his deranged and mutated Vulcomons as his enslavers. His final and glorious goal is the capturing of Etudadorma, and therefore, all of Dimensia 4.

Let us now begin with Trolldar's history lesson of Dimensia 4.

PART ONE: AGE OF ICE
CHAPTER ONE: ANCIENT MAN AWAKES

In the days of ice, before men had time to relax and think about themselves, there were these survivalists in the land called Feriandimal. Every minute had to be spent in finding food, keeping warm, or protecting themselves from the many large and vicious predators. It was a survival time of either kill or be killed. Dimensia 4 went through warm and cool cycles much like earth and now it was in a gradual warming cycle. The ice melted in many regions and the South became lush with vegetation and wild life. The rains were bountiful, and with the ideal temperatures, it became a paradise for all living creatures.

Back in Feriandimal there lived four young Age of Ice adventurers from the southern Camp of Feriandimal, became discontent with life as their fathers knew it. They ventured south, through the mountains and past the ice fields, into this land of paradise. The sun was warm on their backs as they ventured further into this lush land. Soon they had to shed all their winter skin clothing and bathe in the warmth of this sun.

Leaving the mountains, they traveled into the valley floor where they found lush trees and bushes that were filled with delicious nuts and fruit. They saw and caught wild life that was in abundance everywhere they went. They also became aware that they were the only inhabitants in this entire region. They were so overjoyed with their find that they quickly returned to report their good news.

They went straight to the Council of Hunters with their findings. These tribal leaders set themselves up as spokesmen for all of the families in the South Camp. Ohnik, one of the family group leaders from Lochness, was known for his strength and

AGE OF ICE

cunning valor. He was so much wiser than the other hunters that he became leader of the Council of Hunters. The Adventurers told of the warm climate, the beauty and lushness there. They discussed this new event over and over amongst themselves. I will call a meeting of the Council after we have discussed this with our families.

Ohnik,s son , Kuballar, was one of the Adventurers. When they got back to their family cave, Ohnik asked him all kinds of questions and Kuballar gave him a detailed story of the entire trip. That night the whole family gathered around the fire and listened as Kuballar spoke over and over about the beauty and lushness of this new land they had found. He spoke of the plentiful game, the fruit and nuts and to make it more inviting, they found no other inhabitants living there.

That night Ohnik could not sleep. He spent the entire night thinking about what the Adventurers had told them. In the morning he talked this over with his wife, Renick. This was not normal for a caveman, but Ohnik had become a changed man over this last year. He was more considerate of others, particularly his family. She asked him a lot of questions, but in the end, agreed with him. He told Kuballar of their discussion. That night, around the fire, he stood before the fire and spoke, "What my son, Kuballar, here, has told us, is so exciting that I have made up my mind. We are leaving this family cave and moving to this new land. Ohnik thought there would be resistance to his idea, but instead the family got up and started to dance around the fire shouting, "Upah! Wishuga! Upah! Wishuga." He smiled and shook his head in approval and then said, "Nusea hence I will call a meeting of the Council of Hunters and tell them of my decision.

The next morning he sent his son Kuballar and some of the other family member's sons to go out and informed the other Council members of his planned

AGE OF ICE

meeting. They all showed up at the appointed time. Ohnik went before the ritual fire and spoke, "I have discussed the Adventurers' story with my cave families. They were all excited about this new land, so I have made up my mind, my family will leave our cave and travel to this new land. Go to your caves and discuss this with your families and as the nusea rises," Ohnik picked up a stick and drew seven circles in the dirt, and continued, "I urge all of you to come back at this designated time, but those that do, I will expect you and your families to travel with me." They all left and went back to their respective caves.

As the days went by, there was much discussion, both pro and con, for Ohnik's adventure. Those that were not always so successful in the past years in their hunting adventures and some of the families suffered and had bad blood between them. They did not trust Ohnik or anyone else. It was their way. They would sooner land a club on a person than trust in him. Many were suspicious of anything new and thought all new ideas came from evil places. There were many others, however, that had been on many successful hunts with Ohnik and listened to his wise advice. These hunters had always done better. They had avoided internal family fights. Young sons no longer killed or drove out their fathers in order to take over the leadership. There was plenty of food, thanks to Kuballar's clever inventions of the snare and the development of the bone hook to catch fish. Even the women were treated different. They no longer were beaten by their dominant males to keep them in line. Ohnik taught them that a family leader could get their families to do much more with a strange new word that Ohnik introduced to them, love. He showed them by putting his arms around his wife, Renick and giving her a hug. Then he told them that he had assigned her to be leader of the household cave. He further reported that she did a better job than he did and he had more time for hunting and his leadership role. Some of his followers had tried it and found out how successful

AGE OF ICE

it was. Many of these family leaders grew strong respect and admiration for Ohnik. Six nuseas came and went and Ohnik, became apprehensive about who would show up. "After all," he said to Kuballar, "This is a much bigger decision than a hunting trip. If some do not want to go then I will understand." "Don't worry," was Kuballar's reply, "they will all be there. You are a strong leader, and besides, in our story, we told of the beauty and pleasure to be found in this new land, surely that will sway them all to join us." "I hope you're right," replied Ohnik.

On the seventh nusea Ohnik and Kuballar went out on the high ridge to watch the trail. It was just nusea up on and Kuballar yelled to his father, "there, Father, coming up the trail between the two ice field, the families are arriving." Ohnik looked out and sure enough, there they were. They hurried down and got ready to greet their guests. Thirty families arrived for the meeting. He was glad to see so many families had believed in his advice and had come. "After all," he thought, "I have helped many families, including my own, how to treat each other better and have a more successful life because of it." He knew he had gained special powers. It was as though he was in a dream. He had heard and seen these new ideas floating before him, bidding him to accept, and accept he did, for that glowing force in his hands would not let him do otherwise. But who was he to question, for after all, it was working for him and those that he handed it to as well. Just look at what my son and the other three Adventurers have accomplished."

Ohnik greeted them and when they were all settled around the ceremonial fire, he spoke, "My good friends and fellow hunters, I am so glad that all of you came to this meeting. The more families that go south with us the more success we will have. As some of you know The four Adventurers that made this meeting possible are, my son, Kuballar, Joncar, your son, Kibling, Philcor, your son, Pillas,

AGE OF ICE

and Comptes, the son of Jealon, who I might add, did not attend this meeting and has decided not to go. Their return with the wonderful news of their adventure and their great success on this long and dangerous adventure, has only but to convince they should be the ones to lead us to this Promised Land." In his mind Ohnik wondered how he had thought up these last words but he still wasn't aware that a greater force was guiding him.

Ohnik's speech was followed by much discussion. The four Adventurers went around to all the families and personally answered every question they had. As they detailed all the wonders that they saw and lay ahead for the families that go more and more leaders got excited and gave their approval to Ohnik's suggestion. Ohnik then gathered them all back into the magic circle and praised them for their wise decisions. He then drew ten circles in the sand and said, " We gather here on this nusea," pointing to the tenth circle, "and leave on the next nusea of the final preparation. Have all that you can comfortably carry with you for once you arrive, you can not go back for anything. I know some of you must leave some precious things behind but carrying too much on this long journey will be too much of a burden on us all." With those remarks he gave them leave and bid them safe journey to the tenth nusea return.

Ohnik spent the next days packing and preparing for the long journey. He asked many questions about the dangers on route and what to expect. Kuballar answered them with great precision and clarity, so much so, that Ohnik was some what astounded. He was proud of his son. For the first time in the Age of Ice history, that he could remember from fireside discussion of past memories, was there a real closeness between son and father. Usually the father leader was so dominant and cruel that all members feared him. He would maintain this control even as he got older. The only way a younger son could take over leadership was to challenge his

AGE OF ICE

father in a fight. This left either the son or the aging father, either dead, or ejected from the pack. Usually the younger son who studied his father's aging and weaknesses, would gain the upper hand and take over, leaving the weaker father to be ejected from the pack. He was sent into the wild only to be killed by some larger and more ferocious predator. Somehow through Ohnik's dream or vision, he found a new way to lead and maintain family life. It was great to have his son as one of the guides as they journeyed to their new home.

When the nine nuseas had come and gone, Ohnik and Kuballar stood on the ridge overlooking their cave to see if any of the thirty families were coming down the trail. This was, after all, One of the most important decisions any Age of Iceman had to make. Ohnik would not be disappointed if still some families dropped out. While they were gazing off into the distance, Ohnik couldn't help but gaze at his strong young son with admiration. Kuballar looked just like he did when he was that age, many years before, strong, tight muscles, and a sense of well being that nothing could stop him. Ohnik still had some of those feelings but his main skills now were in his head. For some reason that still was unknown to him, he was thinking thoughts way beyond what he ever had thought before. In fact, it occurred to him that those thought were way beyond any Age of Iceman. He knew that this was his destiny and with his young son's strength and vitality, and his aging gathering of wisdom and knowledge the adventure into the green and sunshine had to be a success.

Kuballar also felt a special feeling of closeness to his father. As they continued their scan of the trail, He too observed his father and remembering how loving his father had become, he took the courage and put his hand on his father's shoulder. Ohnik was shocked at first but didn't move. "Wow", he thought, "this is more than any father could expect." Ohnik then put his hand on top of Kuballar's

AGE OF ICE

and they stood in this posture, watching for the arrival of the first families.

Suddenly, as they stood there hand in hand, Kuballar shouted, "Look, Dad, there, beyond that crooked rock, there are people coming up the trail." Ohnik's eyes were not as good as they once were, so he strained to see them. Then in a small blur, he saw the trail filling up with what looked like black dots. Then as they came closer around the last ice flow, he too saw them clearly and grabbed his son and hugged him. "They're here," he cried. With that response from his father, Kuballar replied, "Father, with all the strong leadership you have shown them throughout the years, I did not have any doubts about their arrival for I knew they would not let you down."

Ohnik's cave in Lochness was large enough to hold all of the thirty families. The cave went back into a large mountain covered with ice. There were at least ten different tunnels going back into the mountain. Some had water flowing through, so deep, you couldn't go through. Most were fixed over the years to be a pleasant living quarters. Ohnik and Kuballar had adventured into most of it but it was so long and deep that even they gave up. They cautioned their guest on keeping their family members out.

Soon, they all arrived and gathered in the cave. Both Ohnik and Kuballar greeted them as they arrived. The women greeted each other separately. Even now it was new for them to be social at all. But Ohnik had encouraged Renick to make the first move so she went out of her way to greet each woman and bring them into the cave.

Ohnik gathered all around the ritual fire and greeted them with the wish that their journey would have great rewards. He then assigned rooms for the various families and instructed them in his procedures that they were to follow while in his cave.

AGE OF ICE

He then gathered the women and announced that that from this day forward they would be in charge of the meals decisions, what food, who would prepare it and how it was to be served. "Tomorrow is a new day", he announced, go make your plans and we shall see you in the morning. Ohnik's wife, Renick, was first to take charge for she was already used to her new freedoms. She organized and assigned each family their duties. As time went on she discovered each ones talents and soon the meals went like clockwork. That night they all found their own corner and slept through the night. The next morning Renick had all the women doing their duties and even assigned the older men to special duties. The morning meal was a glowing success. The older men and younger girls cleaned up after the meal.

When all had finished and had time to settle their food, Ohnik called a meeting around the fire. He discussed the journey and had each of the Adventurers explain what they were to expect. Then he assigned the various tasks to each family leader. He assigned duties and responsibilities. The Adventurers went over what each could do and what to avoid on the trip, how to protect the young and old, and what each man must do extra on the trip. "Above all," Kuballar stated, "we are in charge and it is important that you all follow our orders." Ohnik was pleased at his son's last commands, for now he was even more confident that the journey would be a success.

They spent days going over each task and rule until they were satisfied that everyone was ready and knew his task. The next day they spent on inventory of their supplies. Every family set out their supplies and they counted what they had and what they would have to find on the trail.

Everyone was busy running between packs and family members, when Comptes, one of the Adventurer's key leaders, looked down the trail for one last time to where his home and where the rest of his

AGE OF ICE

family decided to stay. As he was staring into the distance, he started to see some small dark images coming up the trail. As they got closer he suddenly realized it was indeed his family. Comptes yelled with joy, "My family, its Jealon, its my father!" They all stopped and looked down the trail. "Sure enough," sounded Ohnik shouted, "I knew he would not let us down. Now our colony is complete." As Jealon and all his families with him approached, Everyone greeted them in their formal Age of Ice tradition. Each male member would approach the outtaguest stand stoic before him, grunt a greeting, usually Upah Wishuga, and then lay down his club in front of him as a gesture of acceptance. Ohnik again broke tradition and spoke, "Jealon, I just want you to know how happy I am that you decided to come after all. Your son, Comptes is an important guide in our journey and your journey with us will make his guidance that much better."

Jealon was shocked at Ohnik's statements. Age of Icemen never spoke their true feelings. They believed that letting them out would weaken them and give the others an upper hand, but Jealon was weary and exhausted and even this gesture seemed to be a good omen.

CHAPTER TWO: THE JOURNEY BEGINS

It took a second nusea to get Jealon's families ready and processed into the colony. Then, on the thirteenth mark in the sand for the rising of the nusea, the thirty-one families headed out to their new destiny and the Promised Land. Their journey led them far to the south, through many ice fields and mountains, through dangerous terrain and floods, until they would reach their goal.

The four young guides had spent many previous days going over their first journey to make sure that they had all the details correct. Kuballar and Comptes led the colony procession and Kibbling and Pillas filled in the rear, to make sure no one was left behind or no rear danger would sneak up on them.

They journeyed down through two large ice packs and into the valley between Mount Doubler and Mount Darkner. There, they passed across to a small inlet canyon by Mount Doubler. There, they had in the

KUPABIN

AGE OF ICE

past, caught many fat kupabins. These large pig like creatures were easy to catch and were filled with meat and fat. Age of Icemen who have lived in frigid temperatures all their existence, needed extra fat to sustain them. This animal was a perfect food. Ohnik and Jealon took some hunters up the canyon. There was a narrow pass that led to large opening. Once they were inside, they realized that they had been driving a herd of kupabin into this canyon and there opening for them to escape. It was a hunter's paradise. Ohnik took his men to the right and Jealon took his men to the left and both closed in. They followed Ohnik's hunting skills which always led to success. Each hunter took his assigned post and closed in as Ohnik directed. With skill they carried out their kill. It did not take long before they had all the kupabin that they needed. They cleaned and cut the flesh into strips. Then they salted the flesh and put them in packs and were on their way back to the colony.

They continued through the valley past both Mount Doubler and Mount Darkner into a very narrow canyon. Even though Ohnik had turned the authority over to the young Adventurers, he could not let up on his leadership role, so, sensing possible danger and it was late time set, he signaled the leaders to stop the colony for the night. They scouted the area and found no cave nearby but Jealon was the expert in finding shelter. He had remembered from a previous hunting trip that there was a large overhang at one ridge and led them right to it. Ohnik was really happy that Jealon had decided to come along for he knew how valuable he would be on the trail.

The overhang was large enough to hold the colony. It would make for tight quarters but it would be adequate. They unpacked and the women, guided by Renick went quickly into action and started preparing the kupabin that the hunters had caught. They had saved just enough fresh meat for the evening meal. Earlier, living near the sea, they learned to

AGE OF ICE

preserve food by packing it in the sea salt. Later on the trail, they found salty rock formations and any thing left over would be salted and packed. As they sat around the fire circle, Ohnik was reminiscing on all that had taken place in such a short period of time. "So far everything was going perfect," he said, "just maybe we will make it to the Promised Land without any serious problems!" But deep down in his inner most thoughts, Ohnik knew this would be a fallacy.

The nights on the ice were extremely cold but they were used to these conditions in their many hunting excursions. Only the women and children had to be given extra attention. They kept their fires burning all night and kept watch on all sides for predators. Their worst suspicions came true. Three swordenfin tubres came into camp from a dark shadow that was cast by a large pillar of rock protruding up from the ground and ice in front of the camp. It was one area the night watchmen could not see. They did not calculate the beast's instincts, though not highly intelligent, their wits were sharpened over thousands of years of practicing for the kill. They saw the dark pillar of rock where they could attack and be unseen. It was close enough that they could jump out, attack, grab some small bodies, and escape before the icemen could counterattack.

SWORDENFIN TUBRES

AGE OF ICE

The three tubres lay hidden behind the dark pillar for a long time, waiting for the right moment to strike. Suddenly as if by signal, they jumped out on each side and darted for the closest prey that seemed vulnerable in the sleeping colony.

The icemen were in family groups, some way in the back of the overhang, and some near the entrance. Some of the women, older children, and older men were chosen to sleep near the fire pit so they could prepare the morning meal, including some fresh kupabin that some hunters had just caught. It might have been this odor of fresh meat that first attracted the tubres. The fire pit was near the entrance and most vulnerable. Ohnik also set his bed near the opening so he would be a middle watch. He was a light sleeper and any small noise or movement would wake him. Suddenly he jumped up just as the tubres attacked. He yelled a shrill warning, one that every iceman knew meant danger. As he picked up his spear, the first tubres came straight at Ohnik. Ohnik , being a master with his spear, drew his spear forward and directly into the mouth of the charging tubres. The spear, with its sharp and jagged stone point, pierced the upper throat. Ohnik lurched forward as hard as his strength could manage, shoving the spear up into the tubres brain. The tubres lurched straight into the air, screeching in agony and fell to the ground, pinning Ohnik beneath him.

The other two tubres saw the closest women and her young son, who had just sat up to see what all the noise was. The tubres snarled at each other and attacked before they could get up and run. The first grabbed the young boy and trust him into his mouth. The boy let out a bloodcurdling scream as the jaws of the tubres closed down on him, driving his sharp teeth straight through the child's body. Soon it was all over and the boy lay limp in the tubres mouth. The second tubres saw his mother, who was gasping in horror at her son's fate, when he too struck her and closed his jaws tightly around her

AGE OF ICE

body. She tried to struggle but the pain was too great and she fell unconscious. Both tubres, having succeeded in attaining their goal, turned and attempted to retreat, where they could enjoy their meal in leisure.

At that moment, some of the hunters saw what was happening and charged the beasts with their spears. The tubres darted away but more hunters appeared. Soon they had the tubres surrounded. Three of the men thrust their spears at the tubres holding the boy. The first spear burst through the tubres's eye and into the lining of his brain. The second hunter sent his spear into the soft part of the tubres belly. The spear penetrated the flesh and entered the inner part of the body, where the hunter turned and twisted the spear until it broke off. Blood and intestinal fluids began gushing from the wound. The third hunter seeing that the tubres still had not fallen and released the boy, thrust his spear behind the ear and directly into its brain where it gave its last struggle and fell still releasing the boy. One of the men ran up to aid the boy but the tubres had done his job and the boy lay dead, torn into pieces.

Four other hunters had arrived and surrounded the last tubres holding the women. This tubres did not succeed either. In his eagerness to escape from the onslaught of the hunters, he dashed head long into a sharp out cropping of rock. The thundering crash knocked the tubres unconscious, knocking the women out of his mouth and thrusting him into the fire pit. The hunters finished him off as sparks flew into the air in the struggle. The men ran over to where the women had fallen and found her rubbing her arm and bleeding. One yelled, "You alright?" Another man helped her up and looked her over but for some puncture wounds and some scratches, she was alright. When she saw the demise of her son, she burst into screaming tears. Renick now came up and helped console her in her grief, another new act of love that Age of Icemen did not do.

AGE OF ICE

Kuballar, who was on watch on the far side, heard Ohnik's warning shouts, and when he arrived he could not see his father and yelled, "Has anyone seen my father?" One of the men, who was treating the wounded women replied, "I saw him on middle watch by that dark pillar in front." Kuballar immediately ran forforward and saw the dead beast on top of his father. The new found love between them caused a strong sense of anguish within him. Thinking that the beast had killed his father, there grew within him a great surge of anger so strong that it turned into enormous strength. This great anger for the beast and his love for his father, caused Kuballar to reach down and with this strength, thrust the 300 pound beast off of his father and the beast rolled aimlessly into the outer ice fields. There between two rock crevices lay his stunned father. Immediately Kuballar shouted to his father, "Are you alright, Father?" Ohnik got up, shook and brushed himself off. Then he turned and immediately hugged his son. "I am glad that you are so concerned about me. Of course I am alright, did you think the great Ohnik would be otherwise?" Kuballar looked at him for a moment, and began laughing as he hugged him back, saying, "Shame on me for thinking otherwise." Then they both laughed and went back to see how the rest were doing.

While some of the men chopped a deep hole in one of the icecaps to bury the young boy, another hunter, named Soothsay, attended the women's wounds. The rest of the women got started preparing the morning meal. The men, guided by Ohnik began planning the days journey down the trail. They were still within their hunting area and most of the hunters were well aware of their surroundings. Tomorrow, however, would be a different story. They would enter no mans land, a place only tread by the Adventurers. Nusea hence would start their official leadership role. Ohnik leaned heavily on Jealon's advice in their discussion of the days journey. He was glad that he had come. Even more important for his son Comptes, who had journeyed with Kuballar to the Middle Earth and the land of glory. In Ohnik's dreams he remembered seeing

AGE OF ICE

the greatness of Comptes and his father. It was here too that he saw a vision of the Promised Land. "Things will be good today for Jealon is with us," he said again to himself. Jealon was credited in saving many lives. He found refuge in many dangerous situations. Many of the caves the hunters used were his discoveries. Then, in the middle of planning, Ohnik spoke, "Jealon is apparent in this discussion here and in your past hunts that you are the one that is superior in knowledge of this land, so now, I appoint you leader of our journey in this land of the hunters. When we no longer have knowledge of where we are, we will let the four Adventurers take over and guide us the rest of the way.

Jealon was shocked that he was chosen leader. After all, he had even refused to go. He knew deep down in his heart that he really had more knowledge of this territory and as much if not more courage than the others, but he was confused, never before had any Age of Iceman given another a compliment and put him above himself. For a moment he stood there dumb founded. Ohnik and the others looked at him and waited. Then he spoke hesitantly at first, "You know I have never been asked to lead but I am sure that I know more about this area and these last mountains than all of you," he now was getting more courage, "why yes, of course I accept and I will not disappoint you." "Good," replied Ohnik, "then it is settled. Let us go back to camp, gather our belongings and then be off to Mount Morgan and and other points as Jealon dictates."

Ohnik was not aware of his leadership skills and his new found gifts he had acquired before all these new events and ultimate decisions had arisen. Gradually he came to realize it was more than just him advancing these ideas. At first it was just like a dream that he saw his destiny flash before him. But the more he thought about it, he came to the realization that it must have been that glowing ball that gave him this power. That strange little glowing ball was there near his favorite hunting

AGE OF ICE

cave. It was almost as if someone had planted it there on purpose so he could find it and pick it up. He was alone with his son on a special hunt. He saw it fall. At first it rolled through some snow. The snow steamed and melted as the ball rolled through it. Then it made a precarious turn and rolled directly into his cave. He became very curious and followed it into the cave. There it sat glowing in the dark. At first he was hesitant to know just what to do. He had never seen anything like that before. Questions started running through his head, "Should he pick it up or would it harm him?" Almost like some force was guiding him. He went over and picked it up. As soon as he did, his mind began to change and he received strange and advanced thoughts that kept flowing more and more through his brain. He sensed his limit and handed it to Kuballar. He held it in his hands for awhile, and he then too started receiving advanced thoughts that raced through his head. Quickly he set it down and joined his father at the edge of the cave. Now, both son and father looked at each other in amazement. They could hardly believe what happened to them. Both sensed the others greatness and growth and felt a sense great fulfillment. "It must be this knowledge that made me choose Jealon just now," he said to himself as he waited for the colony to leave.

Jealon led the colony out of the overhang at the edge of the mountain, down through the two ice fields , then down into a series of rough rocky outcrops and treacherous sharp and jagged ice along the trail. He knew the area well, when to go slow and when to speed up. He had hunted this area many times and camped with many hunting groups. He also knew the worst was yet to come. There was not only jagged ice packs that froze and thawed but sharp jagged rocks, where the demon beast would lay in wait for the fool hardy people, dumb enough to venture into their domain. He only hoped that they would be smart enough and alert so that they could elude these ferocious beasts.

AGE OF ICE

Joncar knew he had other leaders to help him. Joncar was old but equally as knowledgeable. He had seen and actually encountered one of those beasts and he lived to tell about it. So Jealon elected Joncar and his men to guard the rear and he and his men, led the forward thrust of the colony. Ohnik had elected to stay in the middle with his son to guard each side. Philcor and Pillas also paced themselves in the middle to guard more toward the rear.

Jealon and Comptes did not disappoint Ohnik. They followed the trail that led them to the two ridges, where there was a plateau. There, the colony could take a rest and have some food. They spent a short time resting and taking the necessary nourishment. It was important on a rough and long journey like this to keep everyone strong and healthy. One weak link could ruin the whole chain. They left the plateau and Jealon led them down into a very narrow gorge filled with ice caps on both sides. The trail was steep and filled with jagged rocks. If Jealon had another course he would have taken it, but this was the only accessible trail. It was a good thing that Jealon knew this trail, for a novice would surely not succeed here. Here was a prime area for the demon beasts to hide in wait for their prey. He also knew that both Ohnik and Philcor and their sons would guard the women and children well. Plus, he had Joncar and Pillas in the rear. No demon beast would ever sneak by them.

There journey was slow and meticulous. Each step and each turn was recounted by Jealon. He knew how demanding these slippery paths were. He remembered, when he was a boy, he watched his own father fall to his death on those sharp pinnacles lying just below them. It happened in this very gorge. Jealon instructed his men to mark every impassable rock or ridge to help the women and children make a safer journey. In the tradition of the Age of Icemen, if a hunter fell, that was his own fault and deserved not to live, but here, brought on by Ohnik and his

AGE OF ICE

new transformation of caring and love, all this had changed. It was not only Ohnik and his son, for Kuballar had passed it amongst the Adventurer four and their fathers touched it as well. The first adventure and this one would not have been possible if it were not for so many being transformed and advanced in knowledge.

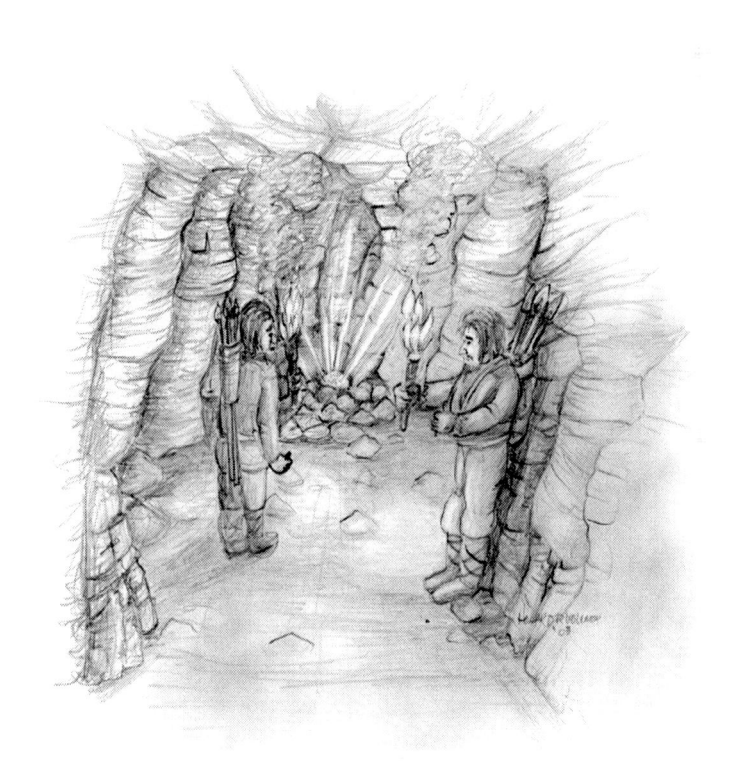

CHAPTER THREE:
THE HUNTER BECOMES THE HUNTED

As the colony edged their way down the slope, little did anyone realize that the swordenfin tubres was not finished with them yet. There was a large herd of them stocking the colony, just waiting for the right opportunity to strike. They were smarter than most beasts and could even communicate through stomping and uging sounds. There were very sensitive levels of stomping and uging sounds, which led to an ever higher level of understanding to the group. One stomp and three ugings meant trouble and they should retreat, two ugings and one stomp meant that it was clear to attack. Each tubres learned all the signals and that's why they were so dangerous. Even now this herd of tubres found out about the dying tubres and they were here for their revenge.

Joncar was on the rear watch and this was good for he had encountered and fought many tubres herds and even demon beasts and Philcor's son was also in the rear with his extra sensing of danger. They were in the right spot in case the tubres actually got close enough for the attack. It was too soon for Pillas to sense danger, so for now all was clear.

The colony climbed down into the gorge. It was almost like ants crawling through a crevice in a large rock. The trail twisted and turned as it worked its way down the sharp rocky path. The pinnacles were so high that they blocked out the sun in some places. It was cloudy today and this meant an even darker decent. It started to snow and Ohnik and his men had to help each child go through the narrow, twisting path. The clouds and snow made it extra cold and they had to put on an extra layer of clothes. This also made the going tougher. Ohnik didn't want anyone to freeze their hands or feet for this surely would hinder their journey.

AGE OF ICE

It started to snow even harder now which made the journey even more treacherous. They had one more straight open area to go through and they would then climb higher to the mountain's pass. It was here that there was a platform, large enough to hold the colony, so they could eat and rest.

Jealon and his men worked their way up the rough rocky path, pounding the sharp edged rocks flat with their clubs so that the trail would be easier for the women and children. They took no chances that a woman or child should stumble and fall on these sharp edges, gashing themselves severely. Age of Icemen normally would not be this considerate, particularly of women, who they found to be a mere commodity to be used and then cast away, but this confrontation with the Glowing Ball of Knowledge, left the leaders with an extra sense of duty and caring. Ohnik's task was to watch over the safety of the women and children. He would send his men back and forth through the colony to make sure everyone was safe and accounted for.

Pillas and his father entered the larger and flat opening in the rear. Suddenly, Pillas's sixth sense kicked in. He shouted to the hunters around him, "Be on guard! There is danger around us." Joncar took two of his strongest and bravest hunters and sent them around to the left of the middle colony and two others to the right. He, Pillas and his remaining men, took cover on each side of the trail and hid behind some ridges. Pillas's fears were not wrong, there, coming up behind them, were ten tubres. He motioned his men to wait. They let the tubres pass in front of them. As the tubres moved well up front of them, Kibbling took out his goula horn and blew a thunderous blast through it. Everyone from the front to the rear of the colony heard the blast and immediately went into action. Ohnik and his men grouped themselves on the outer edges of both sides of the colony. He left some of the men in with the women and children just in case a tubres would slip through. The right and left flank

AGE OF ICE

hunters heard the horn and responded. Joncar was one of the left flank hunters. He was at the far end of the flat opening and Philcor was a little forward and higher up. They both were higher than the rest of the colony and could see the tubres approaching through the snow. Philcor wanted to attack immediately but Joncar pulled him back and said, "Let us not hurry this. Let us alert Kibbling so he can rally the other hunters. Then we will

BEGINNING JOURNEY TRAIL MAP

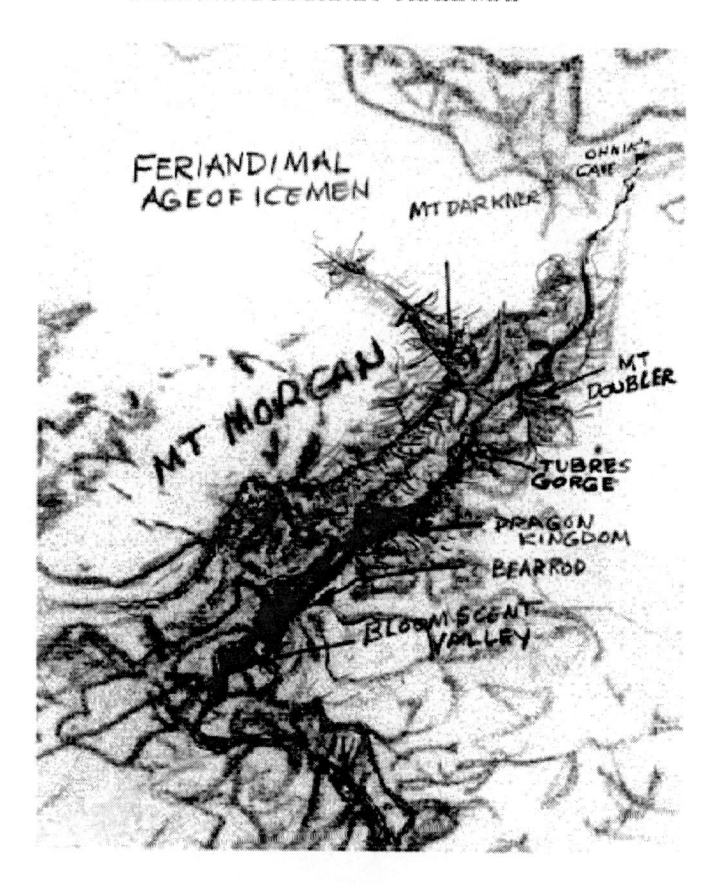

TUBRES CANYON

AGE OF ICE

wait till Kibbling gives the attack signal with his horn. The tubres was closing in and getting closer. They had figured that the ever increasing snow storm would be a good cover for their attack. They were closing in on the colony and now was close to Ohnik and his men.

Kibbling found that everyone was ready for the attack and blew his horn and the hunters began their attack. Before the tubres knew it, the Age of Icemen had them surrounded. As the tubres tried to attack, the hunters pounced on them with spears and axes flying. Two of the tubres tried to escape to the rear where Joncar and Philcor's men were flanked. They raised their spears and axes in readiness. Then as the tubres approached, Joncar saw a large demon beast behind him, hiding in a dark crevice of a large out crop. Quickly he shouted at all the men to duck and the beast leaped over them and straight for the tubres. It really wasn't a fair fight. The demon beast was ready for the fight and the tubres was running in fright and didn't see him coming. It tore the first tubres's throat open with one slash. It quickly leaped over it and pounced on the second, plunging its razor sharp teeth into the tubres's neck. It struggled for a moment and then went limp. As the demon beast stood over his prey, wondering which to eat first. Joncar, Philcor, and the other hunters pounced on the beast with their spears flying and their axes swinging, pounding the beast to the ground. It was a short and deadly battle but the Age of Icemen had the upper hand from the start. The tubres were on an emotional rage and not following their normal precautions. The hunters were trained and alerted to the danger and this gave them the edge of a surprise attack. After it was all over, they gathered the colony in the center of the open flat and took count of everyone in the colony. This meant that Jealon and his men and the forward group would have to retrace their path down the rough terrain again. Joncar and Philcor also came down to where the hunters had killed most of the tubres. It was unbelievable, there were eight dead tubres in the middle, and Joncar reported the death of the other two, plus the killing of the demon beast. Ohnik took this opportunity to speak a rally cry to the colony. He got on a high boulder and spoke, "My good friends! This is surely a sign that this journey was meant to be. We will have great success in our journey to our Promised Land." Ohnik introduced this term for the first time to the colony. He felt stronger and stronger that some greater force was compelling all of them to this new land that waited them. Kuballar joined his father and also spoke to the group, "Yes, Kibling and I can tell you that you will be more than pleased when you arrive at what my father calls the Promised land. Comptes also took this opportunity to talk, "Yes, it is truly as my grandfather would tell me about his vision of what he called Paradise." Ohnik spoke again, praising Pillas's extra senses, "I want to tell all of you that you have our young friend here, Pillas to thank for our good fortune. If it wasn't for his keen senses, there would be many of us dead or wounded by those tubres." Everyone turned to Pillas and through his rough and tattered beard, they could see a bright purple flush on his face. No one had given him praise before. It was expected of every hunter to contribute his talents. If he did less, he was chastised.

They took count and all were accounted for. Only a few hunters had some bruises and cuts from the battle and no deaths. Soothsay helped the men bind their wounds. The leaders gathered around Jealon, for he now was there leader. Jealon looked around at the scene, thought a moment and then addressed the men, "We had planned our arrival at the summit where we could rest and eat but this new event causes us additional problems. We have all these dead tubres to attend to. We must take this opportunity to gather food for our colony. We do not know when we will get this much meat again. We also are not sure if there are more evil beasts, ready to prey on us. We can only hope that Pillas's keen senses will help us." Pillas stepped forward and replied, "I can assure you that there are no other beasts preying on us now." Ohnik came up and said to Jealon, "May I speak?" Jealon replied, "Of course, Ohnik, you always have wise thoughts." Ohnik turned to all the leaders and said, "The hunters must stay here and clean and prepare the dead beast and tubres. What will happen to the women and children? They can not stay here in the open all night. It is too dangerous and cold for them." Jealon thought over what Ohnik had just said and replied, "I have decided that we must split up for the moment. I and Kibling will take half the men with us and take the colony up the ridge to the higher plateau. There they will have shelter and can prepare food for our journey forward to the Promised Land." They all looked at Jealon and then discussed this amongst themselves. They turned to him and nodded in approval. Ohnik spoke, "Yes, Jealon your plan is good. You are becoming an even wiser man than all of us thought." Now even Jealon was blushing with this new attention and compliments. He turned to them and replied, It is so, then. I will depart with the colony and you men will stay and prepare the meat."

Jealon, Pillas, Kibling, selected their men and took the colony up the ridge to the plateau. Ohnik, Kuballar, Joncar, Philcor, and the rest of the hunters stayed behind and started the process all hunter must do after the kill. Over the years they found team work was quicker. Some cut open the animals and removed the innards. Another group skinned the carcasses with sharp, thin stone knives. A third group took the carcass and cut the meat from the bone. Philcor and his men used axes to chop through the bones and separate the different parts. The fourth group cut the meat into long thin strips and handed them to the last group who packed fresh meat for immediate use and salted and packed the rest. When they had finished this task, all joined in and salted and rubbed the hides with a special preparation to cure the hides. They then carefully folded and tied them in carrying bundles. It was

AGE OF ICE

now getting too dark to venture up the trail, so they decided to spend the night in the open, a practice, not uncommon with the Age of Icemen. They gathered all their possessions and placed them in the center of their camp. They stoked the fires they had made earlier and cooked some of meat they had just killed. They were really exhausted and quickly placed heavy fir skins under them and a some others over the top. They curled up inside them like a cocoon and fell fast asleep. All but Ohnik, for his mind traveled back to all the events that had taken place in such a short period of time, and of course, the Glowing Ball of Knowledge. He thought about how much he and Kuballar had changed and some of the leaders as well. Not only did the mental and intellectual level grow in each one who touched it but the influence they were placing on others was astounding as well. His only regret was that he did not take it with him. He searched and searched for it before he left to no avail. He asked all those he knew touched it but no one remembered where it was. He surmised that there were just too many handlers and not enough controls.

DEMON BEAST

CHAPTER FOUR:
SOMEONE HIGHER MUST BE GUIDING THEM

He tried to fall asleep but the thoughts of the ball persisted. What was that strange power it possessed. How all of us change so much just by touching a glowing ball. Kuballar had given it to Kibling. He changed in a strange way. He started to scratch strange signs in his cave. Some of them looked like animals, some looked like a hunting expedition, and another looked like a women with baby. Kibling had never thought those kinds of ideas before. He only was proud of his hunting skills. And look at Philcor and Pillas. Philcor was content to hunt with his knife and spear, now he had to go and invent that awful wicked axe. It could slice a man in two with one blow. Pillas too, he was just an ordinary hunter with ordinary skills, now he has acquired this extra sense of knowing when danger is there, even before it happens. Then there is Kuballar, my son. He would have never thought to gather the four Adventurers together and journey to a distant land. It seemed to Ohnik that some force must have led them there and back, and here we are traveling the same path. Gradually as those thoughts went around and around in his head, he finally fell sound asleep.

In the morning the snow had stopped. It had snowed continually through the night and covered them with a thick blanket. This snow blanket actually helped keep them warm. The scene was filled with sparkling snow and it was as if no one had ever been there but for some bumps in the snow.

Joncar and Kuballar were first to wake up. The sun was just appearing over the rocky ridge. They brushed the snow from their skin blankets and as they saw all the snow sparkling in the nusea, they yelled, "Hufda!" This woke up all the others to the same surprise. All except Ohnik, who was still sound asleep. It wasn't like Ohnik, for he was

AGE OF ICE

always first up and first to go, but no one realized how he had laid awake pondering his many burdens that were resting heavy on his shoulders. Joncar went over and shook him. He jumped up as if in a daze but soon caught himself. "Wow," he said looking at all the sparkling snow, I guess I stayed awake thinking too much last night, I am never last to get up, but this sight is really great." They ate a morning meal, packed their supplies, and newly acquired meat and skins and were off up the steep, rough trail to meet the rest of the colony.

Jealon and the colony made their way up the narrow, rocky trail with out any more difficulty. The leaders set stations and assigned duties to the group. Each family found their own little niche in the cave they found in the wall of the cliff. When each was settled, they came back for assignments. Things were going smoother each day on the trip, thanks, in part, for Renick's new found skills in leadership. Some of the wives of the hunters left behind, were real worried that their husbands were in real danger, but Pillas assured them that he had sensed no danger and they would be safe. With the new found faith in Pillas's extra sensing of danger and Renick's consoling talks, they settled down and went about their regular duties.

Kibling was pleased with himself. He was helping the colony through many ordeals and giving many peace of mind by his calm and persistent reassuring manner. He too wondered why he, after Kuballar had handed him the Glowing Ball of Knowledge, he had attained all these gifts. He now was drawing images on walls of his cave, similar to his own experiences, yet, he knew not why this was happening. It seemed to him some driving force, beyond his own doing, that compelled him to do it. Even now something was stirring inside him, some great drive forcing him to ask these questions and then finally forcing him to chisel them into the stone of the walls where he experienced them.

AGE OF ICE

Kibling gathered various colored clays, red sand, and fire pit charcoal for his colors. He chewed a willow like twig until it had a soft strand like hairs for his brushes. He found his mallet and stone chisel and began carving figures on the wall and coloring them to represent the mysteries of the last days. He didn't understand why he was doing this, it was almost as if some greater force was compelling him to do it. He knew he must transform his experiences into graphic forms. After he was done chiseling the figures, he had his son, Arteson help him brush and dab the colors in the right places, by holding the various pallets up while he painted. He let his son paint some too, knowing how eager he was to help. The pictorial scene was way back in the depths of the cave and Arteson had to hold a torch as well. The newly acquired animals had a lot of fat and this led to an abundance of oil, so they used two other torches and wedged them in the crevices of the rocks. When they finished Arteson remarked how good it was and his father hugged him and said, This is our secret for now, do not tell anyone what we did here." His son promised and they returned to the group in front of the cave.

The women had prepared the meal and they all set in for a well deserved sleep. The night watch took extra care after what they had just experienced. The night was very cold but uneventful. This night Jealon did not stand watch, for he was so exhausted that he fell fast asleep and slept till morning.

The usual events took place in the morning, the older men made a larger cooking fire, the women prepared all the food available to them. This consisted of dried herbal stews, made with fresh meat, and some soft bark and leaves that they found on the way. The younger girls ran errands and prepared shell dishes that they took along for the meals. It was a busy sight. Each had his or her assigned duties and they scurried back and forth trying to get ready for thirty-one family groups. Even with

AGE OF ICE

Renick's skills, preparing for this many took time. As they were busy in their tasks, the far watchman shouted, "Here comes Ohnik and all the hunters." Everyone stopped what they were doing and ran to the edge of the cave. Even some of the men still sleeping jumped up and ran to see. Sure enough, there in the distance came the hunters, carrying their heavy packs, spears, axes, and all their other gear. It was a sight to behold. It looked like an army of ants carrying their own weight or more up the mountain trail. Quickly, many of the men in camp ran down to help. Soon, all the newly acquired meat was safely in camp. As never before, the women met their husbands and hugged them, and told them how worried they were and how they missed them. Each man in his own heart, felt a new sense of pride and belonging.

They all had much to say, Ohnik telling his story of the night in the wild, and the others bubbling over with stories. Not to be outdone, the dwellers in the cave, told their own hair raising stories. It seemed like each one wanted to out do the other. Finally, after much babbling, Joncar raised his voice above all the others and said, "Well, Kibling my son, what have you to say about how you spent your time?" Kibling was stunned for a moment, thinking that he was not that important in his father's thoughts and remembering that he did not want to reveal his new art work. Finally, after quite a while of silence, he replied, Well Dad, if you must know, my son Arteson and I have been deep in the cave recording the events that have happened to us." Joncar looked at his son strangely and asked, "What is this thing you call recording? I do not understand what you mean." Kibling put his arms around his young son, Arteson and hesitantly replied to his father, "Well, its sort of a story that I carve and paint on the cave walls. It is something that I feel I must do since I have touched the glowing ball. Joncar stood stoic for a moment taking into his thoughts all these new ideas, then he said, "Okay, so you and my grandson

AGE OF ICE

have done this recording, you can not hide it from us, show it to us now!" "If you wish, Father, but it is deep in the cave and everyone who is going must take torches along to see." Many of the men around them began to mumble and whisper among themselves. Oxenya asked Ouspa, his son, "What is this thing that Kibling has done that he needs to hide it deep in the cave?" Ouspa replied, "Maybe it is some sort of magic or more of that glowing ball thing they keep talking about," Ohnik sensed their concerns and doubts and said to them, "If you have any concerns, why don't you go to the cave with us and see for yourself what Joncar's son has done"

So all the leaders and the men that were interested, lit torches and went with Kibling and his son Arteson to the cave artwork. Arteson was now really proud that he had helped his father, and as they were walking back to see it, he couldn't help but think, " man, am I glad I went with my dad, after all, look at all the attention it has caused all the men in the colony." They arrived deep in the cave and the men spread out the torches so they could see the images on the wall. To their surprise, There was all the carving that were adorned with colors Kibling and Arteson had made. Ohnik And Joncar looked at them very intently for a long while. Then they started asking Kibling questions about the pictures and what they meant. But many of the others reared back and went face down on the cave floor. They became fearful and murmured to themselves while face down on the ground, "For sure," they thought, "this was some sort of evil or magic." They didn't know what, but they thought it must be bad to be so strange. Ohnik, when he was done questioning Kibling, to his satisfaction, turned to the men and said, "Rise, be not afraid for it is not evil, it is a new way to tell a story. But yes, I tell you that you are right, it is magic, but it is good magic, not evil. This will surely bring us luck in our journey." He now saw that they still remained skeptical and his voice became more forceful and direct, " I, Ohnik, leader

AGE OF ICE

of all the hunts, tell you, you must not be afraid! I tell you, honor and follow Kibling into the new land. Yes, the Promised Land, for surely he has gained special powers that go beyond our thought, but he will help all of you if you follow him." All the men now got up and studied the art closely. Then they talked together in groups, and finally, one man, named Oxenya by name, spoke for them, saying, "Yes, Ohnik, you are right, this is magic, and if you say it is good and that he has special powers, we will follow both Kibling and the other Adventurers into the new land." They all seemed satisfied at what they saw and what was said, so they all returned back to the rest of the colony.

There the men who were, at first skeptical, but now sure, that Kibling did indeed have great magic and special powers, so they went throughout the entire colony, reporting the great magic that Kibling had performed on the cave walls. Arteson, seeing all the honor that his father was getting, came up to him and hugged his leg. Then, Kibling, sensing his sons pleasure, picked him up and held him over his head and saying to all as he passed amongst them, This is my son Arteson! He helped me too and even painted some of the figures. He is magic as well!" Now, Ohnik, watching this historic event, leaned over to his son Kuballar and said, "What great events are taking place, both outwardly and inwardly, since we have handled the Glowing Ball of Knowledge," Kuballar's only comment was, "Yes, Father, This is a great day for us all."

CHAPTER FIVE:
SKEPTICISM & THE GREAT SURPRISE

It was a new day and a new beginning. The leaders spent time, going over the rules and new directions for the various groups. The last encounter was a good warning to take extra precautions. They spent two days on the ledge and in the caves, resting and discussing further details of their journey. There were still those that were leery of change and the aspect of the known adventure. Questoma came to Ohnik with his doubts saying, "Oh great leader, I beseech you, here my plea, for I, and some other men, still have some doubts. Everything is changing so fast and we are used to our old life style, now, you have brought us into this new environment, where we can hardly grasp what is going on. You keep talking about a glowing ball and we know not of such thing." Ohnik listened carefully to his cry and responded, "I know some of you are hurting and confused. It is a lot to ask of so many, to come to a journey that none of you even understand, but you must trust us! Remember all the days on the hunt, when things looked bad, and somehow, we survived. Well we have, not only ourselves and our own strengths, but we have a great, outer force that is guiding us. Don't ask me to explain, for I can not give you an answer. You must trust in me and all our good hunts, and then have faith, that all this will get us to the Promised Land." Questoma was very intent and thought about what Ohnik had said, and finally he spoke, "Your words sound good but I am still not sure that I can convince the others. If we too could touch the magic ball, then maybe we would all believe." Now, Ohnik had a real problem, but he was quick to answer, "Oh Questoma, my good friend, if it were possible I would comply, but, Some of our leaders, I know not who, lost the glowing ball and now, only the ones that gained the knowledge and force from it can advance and lead you. I implore you my brethren, have faith in what

AGE OF ICE

you see and all of us together will reach the Promised Land." He again became more stern in his remarks, "If you and your colleagues do not do that, then you will upset our entire plan and you will be to blame for failure. I do not think that you would want that kind of negative reaction, on the part of the colony, blamed on you and your cohorts. Now go and tell the others and make a real effort to convince them." Questoma was so shocked by Ohnik and that he stammered a faltering reply, "Oh Sir Greatness, the one who brought us through so many hunting tragedies, I beseech you, Please forgive me for doubting you. I will go back and tell the others that we are totally behind you and the young Adventurers." With that, he gave leave and departed.

On the third day Ohnik conferred with Jealon and they both decided it was time to pack up and move out. Jealon gathered all the leaders around the magic fire circle and said, "Now it is time for us to journey forth. We are still in our hunting territory, but soon, we will be into virgin new territory that only the Adventurers know. I am still knowledgeable about this territory, but within the day we will be at the edge of the ice world. Comptes has told me many stories of large green grass areas, large grostiks, blumen bukastiks, plumefrus, and cruntebred, and abundance of animals for food. We know not of these things but have faith and trust that our sons are truthful. You have heard all the stories of magic and new wonders, so have faith in this new adventure, for I promise you this! All that arrive, will be justly rewarded."

There still were many that started murmuring amongst themselves over what they heard. Questoma, to help alleviate more problems, stepped up and asked a leading question, "Most honored Jealon, some of the family leaders still do not understand how, when we leave this familiar and charted hunting area, will we be able to know where we are

AGE OF ICE

going?" Jealon was quick to reply, "Yes, that is hard to understand, for many of our hunters wondered too far from our hunting grounds and we have never seen them again, but I must tell you that with my son, Comptes, it is different. He has acquired extra skills in knowing always where he is at and how to find back. Comptes was, after all, responsible to guide Kuballar, Pillas, and Kibling to this promised land and guide them back safely. He tells me that he stares into the night sky and he can see the many pattern of white lights. He sees these patterns move across the sky, all except one, which is always in the same place. This light and the other patterns help him to see the directions and where he must go. I believe him for if it were not so, how could the boys go all the way that way and return safe? I tell you that he also has acquired a special magical gift."

Questoma tried to convince the leaders of the truth that Jealon was saying, but again they gathered in groups and murmured amongst themselves. There was both pro and con arguments flying back and forth. Ohnik and Jealon began to worry and paced back and forth along the ledge of the overhang. Now, Joncar and Philcor had joined them, for they too were getting worried about some of the family leaders doubts. Philcor asked Ohnik, "Ohnik, I was thinking, maybe we have given these men too much information and they don't understand it?" "Maybe you are right", remarked Joncar, "maybe they will become frightened and take their people back home while they still have a chance." "Yes, you could be right," replied Ohnik, "after all, they have not touched the Glowing Ball of Knowledge and they do not see the world as we see it. yes, maybe we have said too much to them."

The four men paced the ledge of the outcrop while inside the family leaders were still arguing back and forth what they should do. After much arguing, Oxenya, one of the more level headed but always questioning family leaders, came out and

AGE OF ICE

approached Ohnik and Jealon saying with a stern sound in his voice, "I would like to take your sons with me to the family leaders discussion, and then we can decide." Ohnik replied with an equally stern tone, "And to what do you want to say, after all, they have gone where no other Age of Iceman has been and they have come back to tell us about their new found glory. What more do you want, Oxenya?" "Well," stammered Oxenya, "Its just that Questoma has convinced me but there are still some strong dissenters that need convincing. I do not have the words to convince them but if they would hear it directly from these magical and skillful boys of yours, then I am sure they will be persuaded to continue on this journey." Ohnik was first to go up to Oxenya and hug him and said, "Of course you have my blessing, and thank you my friend." Jealon repeated Ohnik's jester and, at first, Oxenya was astonished by the forward moves of affection and jumped back. Ohnik reassured him by saying, "It is alright, Oxenya, this is the new way of our people. We are pleased with your words and this is our way of showing you. Come. Oxenya, Jealon and I will get our sons and you can take them to the family leaders that still have doubts and I know are gifted sons will turn those heads around." "Good," replied Oxenya, "let's go."

Oxenya spent time alone with the Adventurers, questioning them so he was well fortified with knowledge. Then he went back with them to discuss the issues with the dissenting family leaders. Hours past and then toward evening, Oxenya came out with the Adventurers, followed by the rest of the family leaders.

Oxenya asked Ohnik and Jealon if they all could meet around the ritual fire circle, so all gathered there and then Oxenya spoke, "I and your sons talked to the leaders and they asked many questions. Kibling also took us back to his figures on the wall. We now our satisfied and are as one united again. We all feel that surely your sons

AGE OF ICE

have extra powers and possess magic. Jealon, when your guidance is at an end and Comptes and the other Adventurers take over, we will all be honored to follow." "Good," replied Ohnik, "the women have prepared a special feast just for such an occasion. Let us now eat and be festive, for we know not when we will have a chance to celebrate again before we get to the Promised Land."

All the leaders left giving Ohnik and Jealon the gesture of approval. They went back to their respective groups to relay the message. That night there was much feasting and celebrating over the slaughtered beasts. Kibling even took time to introduce them to what he called horn sounds. It was the same goula warning horn but he had made some changes so he could vary the sounds. It was well received and probably the first attempt at music of the Age of Icemen. When the festivities ended each family found their respective corner in the cave for a good night's sleep. They also put extra guards at the entrances. With what had happened, they could not be too careful.

The nusea was just coming up when Comptes went out to check if all went well at the watch. The guards reply positive which was a good change from the past days. He went back and the women were busy with the morning meal. Jealon and Comptes gathered all the leaders for review of tasks, instructions, and any new instructions. After thorough briefing, everyone gathered all the supplies and Jealon led the way down the trail.

The next two days were uneventful. There were no new beasts, no new storms, just up and down mountain passes and through ice packs. This may seem tame to the novice but even to these skilled hunters and their families, this was a challenge even without some unforeseen evil.

On the third day Jealon led them up to the high trail that is the last hunting frontier. It was a

AGE OF ICE

steep and rocky trail with sharp, black jagged rocks. At the second to last summit, there was a flat wide opening where they could stop and rest. While the rest were enjoying refreshments, Jealon took Comptes aside and said, "Son, this is as far as I have traveled. It is up to you and the other Adventurers now so I am now officially turning my leadership over to you." Comptes replied, "Thank you Father, have no fear I will do a good job of guiding the colony."

Comptes was in the lead and he led them higher and higher to the top of a pass, just east of Mount Morgan. Now it was even past the last ice pack, and because they were so high, there was still snow all around them. The rocks got even more sharp and rugged and the trail filled with steep inclines. There really wasn't a trail to follow, so Comptes was following his instincts. Jealon even began to question Comptes about his choice of trails, saying, "Son, are you sure this is the right trail?" Even Ohnik came up to me and asked me what you were doing." Comptes just continued on his course and replied, "Yes, Father, this is the right trail. Last night I went out and checked the sparkle reflects. It was very clear so I could find all the sparkle reflect patterns and that stationary one to coordinate and correct my directions. When we get to the top, you and all the colony will have a big surprise that will make you all happy."

So on they trudged. Some fell and got cuts from the sharp rocks, Ohnik yelled out, "Jealon, Comptes, we must stop and rest." Comptes in his jealous quest to show them some glimpse of utopia, was scurrying up so fast that he forgot that there were women and children who needed extra care. Comptes stopped for a moment and replied, "I am sorry, yes we can stop at a clearing, just up ahead." The clearing was just a short ways up and they all stopped for a well deserved rest.

They were happy to stop and rest. The leaders took out the cured strips of meat and a few other herbs

AGE OF ICE

that Soothsay and his men had gathered and passed it around to all the families. There was plant, called toogagood. It was an ice plant, half mushroom, half bread like plant. It was a plant that they found on the way and they used it for carbohydrate consumption. After sufficient time to rest and time to eat, Comptes found the highest rock, climbed up and spoke to the colony, "I want to say how happy I am that all of you were so patient with me and did such a good job on the trail. I know, some of you fell and hurt yourself, but I promise you, there is just a little more hard work and we will all see things that will make us filled with joy and happiness." The entire colony seemed filled with exuberance, after speech Comptes had just made. So they all gathered there belongings on their backs and were off, following Comptes and Jealon.

Hours later and still light, they came to the top of the mountain pass. There was a large cave and an open flat area at the base of the cliff. It was almost as though Comptes had prepared it for them ahead of time. All the leaders were now used to their camping and lodging routine, so they immediately went into action, directing the various family groups to appropriate shelter in the cave. Everyone got their assignments, the women from Renick and the men from Ohnik. When everyone was settled, Comptes and Kuballar led Jealon and Ohnik away from the flat area to a craggy ledge. Ohnik was tired from the many hard days climbing up and down the rough trail. He looked at this rough terrain and asked, "Why are you taking us to this awful looking place? Do you think that we haven't seen enough of these rocks?" Kuballar sensed that his dad was exhausted and young people forget that older peoples energy runs out faster than theirs, so he quickly replied, "Father, just bear with us just a little longer and both you and Jealon will not be sorry you did." Jealon too was exhausted and short of patience and responded to Kuballar's comment, "And tell me, by the hairs of the biggest demon beast,

AGE OF ICE

what is so important that it couldn't wait till nusea hence?" Now his son, Comptes replied, "I know you are both exhausted from the last two days, but because we both love you so, we wanted you to see this , before anyone else." Both older men begrudgingly followed their sons through the craggy ridge. At first it looked like they were going to climbright over the sharp rocks, but Comptes's uncanny memory, found a small, flat opening that led to the edge of the cliff.

Kuballar told both men to close their eyes and the sons led them to a flat spot at the very edge of the cliff. Kuballar said to them, "Okay, open your eyes and look down." They opened their eyes and before them were strange things they had never seen before. These strange things stuck out of the rocks and went up toward the sky. In the middle were large sticks that propelled them to the sky. On top of the sticks were great big flat things hanging all around and covering the top of the stick. Ohnik and Jealon looked in astonishment at the scene below and Ohnik asked, "What are those things?" Kuballar replied, "Those are the green things that we told you about." Comptes broke in, "This is not much! Come through here and let me really show you something." He led them around some more rocky ridges to a larger opening and there below was a large green valley. The sun was brightly shinning on the valley floor, brighter than they ever had seen the sun before. "There," said Comptes, "This is the land of green that I told you about. This is what our new home will look like." Both Jealon and Ohnik were speechless. Then Jealon stammered, hesitantly but loud, "Oh my! Great hairs on a beast! Oh great ice packs! What in the world is that?" Comptes put his arm around his father's shoulders and said, "I told you this is just part of our new home. It is the land of plenty, a place you will find so wonderful, you will not want to leave it." Ohnik was so taken back by the scene that he was speechless for a long while. He thought to himself that this must be what Kibling was

AGE OF ICE

describing to him and it is only a half a mountain away. Then he finally spoke, "Is this the Promised Land?" "No, Father, we have a long way to go to get to our final destination, but it is just like the place that you now call The Promised Land," Kuballar told his father as they too were arm and arm enjoying the beautiful view. "You know Father," Kuballar continued, "this is why we were all so excited when we first got back to Feriandimal. I could hardly hold myself back with the joy of viewing and experiencing this beauty. This is why I was so insistent on all of us coming here. When you finally get to your Promised Land then I am sure you will feel the same way."

As they were returning to camp, Comptes and Kuballar told their fathers not to tell anyone of what they had just observed. "And why not?" remarked Jealon to his son. "Because, Father, it will upset the camp too much. You saw how many of them acted just a few days ago, this surprise, so soon, would maybe put them over the edge." Ohnik thought on this as they were walking and spoke up saying, "You know Jealon, I think he's right. They are going on the faith of the Adventurers now, let them surprise the colony at the right time." "Thanks, Father, you will see we are right," remarked Kuballar. They returned to camp and joined in on their regular duties.

That night both Jealon and Ohnik could not sleep. Thoughts kept going through their heads. Ohnik tried to envision what it would be like with no ice caps or freezing winds, just warm weather? What kind of animals would they hunt? Would there be enough caves for everyone? Jealon thought of the green grass. What it would be like to run through it? Would it be sharp and cutting or soft and pleasant under his feet? Were there enough animals to feed everyone? Were there evil people there ready to kill them? Over and over these thoughts went through both their minds. Finally, after what seemed like hours to them, they fell sound asleep.

KUBALLAR'S SURPRISE

CHAPTER SIX:
THE PLAN, NO ICE, AND THE GREEN REWARD

The next morning was the day of a new beginning. The colony no longer could depend on their old unwavering ones, Ohnik and Jealon. Now, they were dependant on the four young Adventurers, Comptes, the path finder, Pillas, the predictor of danger, Kibling, the creator, and Kuballar, the leader and director. Although the colony had accepted the Adventurers as gifted and possessing magic, there were still some who had doubts. "After all," said Ouspa, the doubter and tracker, even I have more experience than those boys. They are too young to lead. Something surely will happen bad to us! You'll see!" Ohnik heard some others too, mumbling in corners, so he told the four sons, "go back to the look out and make some definite plans you can present to the family leaders. I will speak to them in the meantime and prepare them for your leadership."

Ohnik called a meeting of all the Age of Icemen in a final conference, while the four Adventurers made their final plans. He called on Joncar, Philcor, and Jealon to give testimony and support on behalf of their sons. They each spoke about the their sons adventure through what his son had told him, so each had a slightly different story to tell. Jealon was first and said, "I must admit that I was skeptical at first, for as you know, I almost did not go on this journey with you. But now, I have seen my sons talents and realize that with out his special gifts, he could not have found there and back. Philcor too, spoke of his son's talents and how they will help all the colony guard against approaching danger way before it arrives. Ohnik also gave testimony about Kuballar's leadership skills saying, since I have seen my son on this journey I am amazed how he always comes up with the best solution for every problem, no matter how difficult. Each speech helped the crowd feel more confident. Meanwhile, Kuballar, obeying his father's wishes, took the other three Adventurer and

AGE OF ICE

ventured back to the ledge, overlooking the valley below. In the distance, the nusea was shinning on the trees and greenish purple fields below. It was a very long distance and the naked eye really could not make out those details clearly, but in their memory of it, they saw it clearly. They just stood there and stared for a long time, finally Kuballar said, "Men, you know what joy the colony will all experience once they get there, but as you know, there are still many obstacles along the way. There are mountains ahead of us that have no trails, only jagged rocks and steep sides to it. If it were not for Comptes, we would not have found down to the valley below. So we will depend entirely on you, Comptes. I hope you got your directions from the sparkle reflects, so you can guide us down the right path. "Yes, Kuballar," replied Comptes, "it was clear last night and I saw all the groupings and the still one. Also remember that I have a good memory. I can still see every jagged rock on that mountain. Each one has its own shape and that will also help guide me."

Pillas spoke up saying, "Don't forget that two headed monster half way down the mountain side. He has his own domain and will let no one through." "yes, you are right," replied Kuballar, "we were lucky for there were only four of us and thanks to you alerting us of his danger ahead of time, we were able to sneak around him, undetected. But how do we get a whole colony by his kingdom and Bibutsakufascorchum, that fire dragon, undetected?" They again, looked out over the ledge and contemplated their problem. Then Pillas meekly answered, "Well you know I will certainly give all of you forewarning. The plan is up to you." "Yes," replied Kuballar, "but we still don't have a plan." Kuballar turned to Kibling and said, "Kibling you are our creative master, why don't you conjure us up a plan?" Kibling thought for a moment and replied, "Well, Kuballar, if creativity was that simple, the whole of all existence would be living in utopia, but unfortunately, it relies on sudden flashes of

AGE OF ICE

insights. These flashes come, when I least expect them. However, since my touching the Glowing Ball of Knowledge, I have them more frequently, but you, Kuballar, you have also touched this ball and are our leader, so why do you not get an insight into our problem. It all most seemed like all of a sudden their was building, tension even inside the Adventurers group. But, unbeknownst to them, Trolldar was orchestrating there action, so it would come out to be a favorite able conclusion. Suddenly, even Kibling continued, "By the mouth of the fiery dragon, I have the solution. We will depend on Pillas to give us an early warning. I and Comptes will plan together how we can use the Age of Ice leaders and hunters to, either stand ground, or fight and divert attention away from the main colony, as it slips by." Kuballar thought on this a moment and replied, "Yes that is a real good and creative plan. I knew you would come to our rescue, but we must still refine the details, as to how it will actually work." They all agreed on the plan and spent many hours discussing how it would actually work.

Kuballar, the leader, directed their attention to another problem, saying, "We will also have to have a plan when we reach the Megar Flats. Remember those many armaflorvias that attacked us from the crevices of the jagged cliffs. Then, later we must find a way to fend off the sky beasts between Becaris Flats and Muchohites Canyon. As I am sure, Comptes is well aware of the fact that Megar Flats has very few woods or hiding places. We have our work cut out for us in order to keep the colony safe from all those preying monsters."

They again, went into conference and debated all the pros and cons of many solutions, without coming up with a viable answer. Finally, Kibling turned to all of them and said, "Look, as I have said earlier, creative ideas don't just come when we want them. They will come when the time is right. My proposal is to concentrate on the immediate

AGE OF ICE

problem, namely, the two headed dragon. Let us wait till these other problems come closer to us. Then, I am sure, we all will have plenty of insights, for didn't we all touch the Glowing ball of Knowledge." Kuballar sensing Kibling's great insights commended him for it and said, "We have talked enough, let us go back before the colony gets restless, for now we at least have a good outline plan for our trek down the mountain and at least, some idea of a solution for that two headed beast." They all agreed and headed back to the conference that Ohnik was holding.

When the Adventurers got back, Joncar was delivering an exciting description of the Adventure as seen through his sons eyes. When he finished, Ohnik interrupted the meeting and gave homage to Joncar's speech and at the same time announced, "Here are our leaders now," and pointing in their direction as they approached. "Now they will tell us what's in store for us." He took his son, Kuballar and led him to the front of the gathered men and said, Now my son will inform you on all the details of our coming journey."

Kuballar stood up on a flat rock above the gathered leaders and started his speech, "Men, you are about to journey into an experience none of the Age of Icemen have ever encountered before. It will be a journey you will not regret. The land is warmer than any of you have ever thought possible. There are green, red, and purple things sticking out of the ground, we called grostiks, some were tall and some short and round. There are things we called blumen that had many different colors and smelled really good. On some of the grostiks there were things we could pick and feast. There was an abundance of animals and birds that were just waiting to be caught. yes, the four of us who journeyed there found it so inviting and that is why we urged our fathers and you to come on this journey. Not all has been easy and smooth on our trip, and I must caution you," Kuballar was now talking slow

AGE OF ICE

and deliberate, "there still are perils yet to come, and just maybe, some of these perils may even be worse than the ones we have encountered so far." He stopped a moment to let the leaders think about what he had just said and then continued, "But fear not, for we have been planning and discussing these perils together and we have come up with plans that will keep us all safe from any of these perils." He stopped again to see the reactions on their faces. Some were even smiling, but others had frowns on their face, for they thought all the perils were behind them. Then he said, "Yes, some of you, I see are worried, but don't be, for our plan is to assign each one of you a task and based on your many talented skills, we should have no trouble outsmarting the most ferocious beast that is in our way." This time when he stopped and looked at the men, most seemed relieved at what he had just said and he continued, "Pillas has extra ordinary abilities to sense danger way before it happens. He will tell us long before any beast approaches and then we can prepare and be ready for him."

He was about to explain the first perils, when one vocal hunter named, Ouspa, shouted, "What are these perils you talk about?" The crowd immediately caught the fever and started yelling, "Yes, what peril? Tell us, what peril?"

Ohnik, sensing things were getting out of hand, stepped up and shouted, "Men, quiet! Fear not! Our courageous young sons went there and back and if they have a good plan, let them tell us." Immediately the crowd quieted and Kuballar continued, "The first peril is something you are already used to. There is no trail down the next side of the mountain and it is filled with very sharp and rough rocks. With so many young and old in the colony, this will pose a problem. To solve that problem, we have assigned each leader and family leader, to a group of families and some individual families to watch and help. Each of you men of the hunt and even some of you who belly-ached, are used to this

AGE OF ICE

kind of terrain, so you can help by watching them, guiding them, and showing some, how to do it. You can do this first, by watching and guiding the older people and very small children, and second, by showing the older youth how to do it, soon most will learn and be on their own."

He stopped again to see their reaction to his comments. Most of the men were pleased with what they heard and Kuballar went on, "The second peril is far more dangerous, but here to, we have an excellent plan. When we reach the mid point of the mountain decline, there is a large two headed monster we have named Bibutsakufascorchum. he thinks he owns the territory half way down the mountain as his kingdom. he rains fire on anyone who invades his territory. The four of us escaped because Pillas warned us way ahead of time and we had time to sneak past him. Although we saw him twice, he did not detect us."

Most of the hunters looked at Pillas and shook their head in approval, but, Ouspa, the boisterous one, shouted out, "How big is he?" Kuballar replied, "He is three sizes larger than the demon beast and double as dangerous." Ouspa, who was one of the hunters known for tracking and sneaking up on his prey without being seen, always felt that he should be picked to help as a leader. He resented those that had touched the glowing ball and now so many new and advanced ideas. He would find any reason to insult or disrupt the leaders and put importance on himself. Here too, we find him trying to discredit Kuballar and drive a wedge between the main leaders and the family leaders. Ouspa stands up again and asks, "Our hunters have a hard time defending themselves from the anger and force of the demon beasts, how do you expect them to defend against such a large and ferocious beast as you are describing here?" Now the crowd got boisterous again and shouted, "Ya, how we defend? Ya! How we defend? Tell us now! Tell us now! Tell us or we go back! Muga Puh! Muga Puh!"

AGE OF ICE

Ohnik was just about to step in and settle the group, when Kuballar raised his voice to a high level and raising his both hands above him and spoke, "Fear not, for we have worked out an outstanding solution that all of you will agree to." He knew he really didn't they hadn't really formulated a detailed plan, but now he knew he must come up with one fast. He twirled the thoughts around in his head quickly and continued, "My fellow Age of Icemen, you have a grand tradition of successful hunts. We also have a large colony of brave men. We can not sneak the large colony through Bibutsakupascorchum's kingdom without being detected, but we have a plan. We divide the hunters into three large diversion teams to intercept the dragon. When he closes in on that team, the second team distracts the dragon and it chases them and so on until the dragon is tired. Then we will move in and kill the beast. While this is going on, the dragon will be so preoccupied with the three diversion groups that he will not detect the protector group, guiding the colony past his kingdom, to safety down in the lower canyon."

They all stood stunned! Even Kuballar was amazed at what came out of his mouth. The other Adventurers looked at each other in amazement, and asked each other where Kuballar came up with all the right solutions. Ohnik, feeling a great sense of joy, jumped up on another high rock and proclaimed to the group, "You see! I told you not to worry, that these Adventurers are the best! They were there and knew the perils, they planned a brilliant course of action and now all we have to do is carry it out." Ohnik was now feeling even more confident and added, "Okay men, do you Age of Icemen think your up to it?" with that all the men got up and shouted over and over, "Hig Pu! Hig Pu! Hig Pu! Hig Pu!" All raised their fists in victory shouting, "Upah Wishuga! Upah Wishuga!" and ended with "Butah Mongo!" Even all these accolades caused Ouspa to keep quiet for the moment.

AGE OF ICE

They all met in their respective groups and made the necessary plans and assignments for the journey ahead. The women had a special meal of fresh meat and herbs which added to a more relaxed feelings. They had some story telling by the older men and Kibling played his horn. A few men had made some drums of dried skin and beat them to his music, while few young children danced around the ceremonial fire. They all turned in early, except for the guards, for they knew they had a hard day ahead.

In the morning, everyone seemed excited to be on the road to a new land. All the worries and fears seemed to be gone for the moment and everyone seemed upbeat. The leaders were well versed the day before, so they immediately went into action, assigning tasks and appointing men into their proper work groups. Ohnik and his leaders took their respective positions and the Adventurers decided to space themselves throughout the entire colony line. Comptes was in the front, Pillas in the rear, and the other two spread out in the middle. This way, they could alert each other if trouble in any sector of the colony.

Down the trail they went, Comptes now leading with Pillas and Philcor, making up the rear flank. The first day went well with only a few people falling on jagged rocks and cutting themselves. Soothsay and his helpers were always there to help with the wounds. Kuballar was in constant contact with Comptes to make sure they headed in the right direction. Comptes sent word to him that he was indeed on course for he saw all the familiar land marks he etched in his mind on their first adventure. They stopped for a break in an open area, so the colony could catch their breath and the women had packed refreshments that were passed around. Kuballar came up to where Comptes was sitting and asked him if what he heard from his messenger was accurate. Comptes replied to his concerns pointing to a rock ridge and saying, "Do you see that rock ridge that looks like a dragon's head?" Kuballar

AGE OF ICE

looked intently. He stared for a moment not seeing it and asked, "Where did you say?" Comptes replied saying, "Up there, look up higher Kuballar!" Kuballar looked more closely to where he was pointing and replied, "Oh yes, now I see it. Wasn't that the opening to the dragon's kingdom, where we saw old Bibutsakufascorchum the first time?" "Yes indeed," said Comptes, "we are right on course, ole man!" Kuballar put his arm around Comptes's shoulders and said, "With all the twisting and turning we were doing and the high jagged rocks that all looked alike to me, I thought we were lost. But I'm sure glad your leading this colony with your superior navigational skills. If I were leading we would have been totally lost." "Thank you," said Comptes, "I take pride in my skills and I am learning more every day." Then Kuballar changed the subject and said, "Comptes, we must find a place to spend the night, soon. We are close to the dragon's kingdom and we must gather all the hunters and leaders together so that we can make our final plans to get the colony safely past the dragon." "You are right, Kuballar, and I know that is your responsibility and that you are concerned. We are in luck there too, for I remember that there is a large flat area just this side of that dragon head rock. I think there is a cave there as well." Kuballar replied, "Good, let us tell the leaders before we leave here of our plans. "The leaders went through the entire colony, checking every family group. Then they met to report that all the family groups seemed to be in relatively good condition. Comptes gathered all of them around him and said, "Men, we are approaching close to the kingdom of the dragon. It is very important that all of you get assigned to one of the three groups that Kuballar told you about in our plan. Each of you must understand your individual responsibilities in order for this to work. There is a large, flat clearing with a cave up ahead. We will camp there for the night and then, we can assign and go over the strategy of this plan, so each of you will know precisely your task in this plan." All the leaders went away with a

AGE OF ICE

greater sense of importance and responsibility. This alone gave the colony, a better chance against their huge fire spurting dragon.

Comptes's navigation was right on his target. Early that afternoon, they arrived at the open, flat area and found the cave. The setting up of camp was routine by now, with everyone having a special duty to perform. While they were doing their various tasks, Kuballar and the other Adventurers called all the hunters and leaders together for the strategy meeting. They had to wait for some to finish their tasks, but soon, all were gathered in a circle around Kuballar, and he began, "Men, as you know, we have never encountered a beast like this before. Many of you might die trying to divert this monster from our colony. So therefore, I am going to ask my father, Ohnik, to stand foreword and ask for volunteers to lead the three diversion groups.

Ohnik stepped up and Kuballar took him aside for a minute to upgrade him on the plans. Then Ohnik stepped foreword and spoke to the group, "Men, as many of you have witnessed, hunters are killed in the pursuit of their prey. These men are proven heroes and remain in our thoughts and hearts. There are many of you out there that have also killed the fiercest of beasts and are here today. Let those brave men now step foreword so we can form our first leading diversion group."

There was an awful quiet for awhile. It seemed even though, there were brave men in the group, none wanted to be the first to volunteer. Each looked at the other and some talked amongst themselves. Finally, after many minutes of faltering and mumbling, Philcor stepped foreword and spoke, "I and these many hunters in my group will volunteer for the first group to lead the diversion team. "Good for you, Philcor! You and your men are skilled with the axe and will be a real asset in the fight of this dragon," Ohnik remarked. He made sure everyone heard him give Philcor and his men compliments and

AGE OF ICE

then asked, "Do I hear more voices volunteering or have you suddenly become cowards?" Joncar got almost purple in his face and turned to his men, for a short discussion. He then stood up and remarked, "No one calls Joncar a coward, I and my men will form the second diversion group." Ohnik patted Joncar on the shoulder and said, "I know that you and your many men would not be cowards and that you would stand strong with us. I have discussed this with Jealon and the men in both our groups will make up the third diversion group. Kuballar, Kibling, and Comptes will form the protector group by selecting hunters from the rest of the colony and they will plan their strategy. We will need Pillas in our diversion groups so he can give us warning. Now let us divide into the three groups and make final plans as to how they were going to divert that dragon and get the whole colony through, without being detected." Kuballar reminded them that Pillas was a real asset and help to know where the dangerous dragon was long before he knew you were here. After long discussions, that went back and forth, they finally felt they all had a workable solution.

They went back to the colony and all celebrated after they ate, around the ritual fire circle. Kibling again played, what some thought was a magic horn, others joined in pounding on skins stretched over anything they could find that was hollow inside. Others chanted and danced around the fire. Today it was a time to celebrate for they were rewarded with no snow, and the women picked herbs, and some kind of food off of green, round grostiks. Some of the young people began to sing of large colored grostiks that were growing out of the rocks and strange colored things that Comptes called blumen. They had an abundance of wood for their fires. No traveling on and on, looking for wood. With the easy access of wood and fresh food, it brought joy to all their hearts and the tension and suspicion was gone. Even Ouspa sat in a corner and was seen

AGE OF ICE

smiling and the thought of the hostile dragon didn't seem to even enter their mind this night of jubilation. Gradually the jubilation wore down and all found places for a good night's sleep. Only those who were elected to be on watch and Kuballar, were awake on this grand and glorious night.

Kuballar could not sleep for it all of a sudden hit him that he, and he alone, was responsible for the safety of the entire colony. He knew what a ferocious beast that dragon was. He also knew the skill and tenacity of the hunters. But then on the other hand, Kuballar had seen the dragon shoot fire out of his nostrils and scorched grostiks many lengths away and he also had two heads of fire and again his mind dwelt on the enormous size of this beast. He only hoped, that his new found insights, from the Glowing Ball of Knowledge, would be enough for this gigantic task. So far his plan seemed sound. Even the older leaders and hunters approved and made their own plans accordingly. These thoughts made him feel better but as Kuballar lay in the dark more questioning thoughts ran through his mind, "What if that demon, that fire blowing, two headed dragon, all of a sudden decided on a better plan. After all he had charted a large kingdom for himself and lived here for no one knows how long. He must have fought and won all his battles with his enemies so how can we think that we have the power over him." It seemed like a loosing battle in his mind, but their was a guiding force above him. It was Trolldar's assignment to watch the colony, particularly when in trouble. Now for sure Trolldar sensed that Kuballar had too many doubts and not enough self confidence, so he took control of Kuballar's mind and projected happy and pleasant thoughts of his encounter of the Glowing Ball of Knowledge and all the growth that his mind had attained. Suddenly, Kuballar got a pleasant smile on his face and he fell fast asleep. With his job complete, Trolldar whisked away into the beyond, to attend another, more pressing calling.

AGE OF ICE

Now, only the night watch, stood gazing out at the night beyond them. The night was clear and far Age of Icemen were used to. The nooma reflect spoke loud in the sky, shining its glowing light on the rocks and grostiks before them. Maybe this also was a part of what was waking within these Ancient Icemen, a sense of dance, music, poetic beauty, and above all, a sense of newness of being.

CHAPTER SEVEN:
RONDEVOUS WITH THE DRAGON

It was almost morning and the guards were happy their shift soon would be through. The night was uneventful but the morning soon heard voices as the women were up preparing the morning meal and the older men assigned to stoking the morning fires. They couldn't help but stop and gaze at the morning sky. Some of the women stopped to a see the nooma reflect setting on one side of the mountain and the cracking rays of the nusea, breaking their scarlet and oranges, through the crevices of the rocks. It was a sight to behold for it was something none of the people of Feriandimal had ever seen before. There even was heard some "uuhs" and "aahs" as the workers watched this dazzling display that nature was unfolding to them. This also got some of the hunters and leaders attention as well and they too stood a enjoyed the morning display.

It was now light and Pillas sent some of the hunters out to check the area for dangerous predators. He felt a little uneasy and didn't want to take any chances. As he was selecting the hunters, Kuballar whispered in Pillas's ear, "This would be a good time to let Ouspa get involved and feel more apart of the action." "Good idea," whispered Pillas and the next name on the list was Ouspa. "Yes, sir, how can I be of service," asked Ouspa. Pillas replied, "Ouspa, you are noted to be the best tracker and can sneak up on anything without them detecting you. I want you to lead the hunters out and see if there are any predators roaming about that could harm the colony. I have this strange feeling in me and when its there, there is usually danger lurking about." Ouspa felt honored and took the men and left on their scouting expedition. In the mean time, Kuballar got the leaders of the three diversion groups to go over their directions and plans. He wanted to be sure his insights were correct. As

AGE OF ICE

the three groups were going over their plans, Kuballar took the other three Adventurers and they left to check out the entrance of the dragons kingdom. As they were journeying down there, Kuballar expressed his desire to stay where they were an extra day or two so they would have enough time to prepare properly. The other three thought it a good idea as well.

They reached the gates and then Pillas realized what was bothering his warning zones in his body and he remarked as they stopped at the gate, "You know I sent the hunter to check for predators, but the real problem that has been bothering me is that I sense something is really wrong inside the dragon's kingdom." Then Kuballar quickly asked, "What could it be?" I don't know but we must sneak in there and find out."

They decided that this was the only way to settle Pillas's warning zones, so Comptes led them past the large pillars. These pillars to them, represented the dragon's gates. It really wasn't a gate or a carved likeness of a dragon, but as the shadows, cast their dark images on the pillars, it seemed an enough likeness to actually represent the dragon that they had seen below.

Now inside the gate, they slowly made their way through a rocky chasm, and into an open area that once was a forest. Kibling looked shocked as he gazed at the scene and said, "This once was filled with grostiks as far as the eye could see. Now look at it! There is nothing but burnt and black sticks as everywhere. What would cause this demon to destroy his kingdom like that?" Kuballar, appealing to Kibling's creativity remarked, "Your right, it surely doesn't look as we once saw it, in fact, it looks down right evil. This surely must have been the work of Bibutsakufascorchum." As far as they could see, the land, rocks and grostiks were scorched with fire. They walked carefully around the edges of this domain, so they would not be

AGE OF ICE

detected. Pillas, sensing some new danger said, "Something really got him mad, I can feel it." "What is it?" cried Kuballar. "I sense an even greater danger. What it is, I do not know, but I am sure that we must go back immediately and alter our plans. Kuballar and the others thought on this and decided that it was paramount that they return and reorganize the three diversion groups.

As the Adventurers returned to camp, Ouspa and his hunters had reported no threatening predators in the area and they had good luck in the hunt. They were in the process of cleaning and preserving their catch and storing it for the journey. The women and older men were packing up for the next trek through the dragon's domain. Kuballar went straight to Ohnik. "We must talk," he said excited. Ohnik responded, "What is it that has you so excited, son?" Kuballar's eyes were now enlarged as he spoke, "The dragon's kingdom is all scorched and we're not sure, but Pillas senses that there might be an even larger enemy dragon that Bibutsaku-fascorchum has been attacking. We must all meet to rethink our plans." "Oh my Gupah, a Hig tumon!" was Ohnik's astonished reply, "Yes, I will call all the hunters and you tell all the leaders."

They all gathered and Kuballar told them of what the Adventurers had just discovered. "We must stay the night and prepare for this new problem," Kuballar replied to them. Some again began to murmur and some talked of returning. Ohnik reminded them of the heroes of past hunts and asked them, "Are you heroes or do you want to be thought of as cowards?" With those remarks they all went into discussion as to what plan was right. The discussion went on and on and finally Kuballar stopped them and spoke, "Look men, I've been listening and thinking, we have three diversion teams. Why don't we plan so that we keep circling and confusing the two dragons. Then finally, we will close in closer and closer until they finally meet each other, then, one of them will kill the other and we will kill

AGE OF ICE

the remaining and now, exhausted beast." Again, the words came out as a surprise, both to the men in the planning group, and also to Kuballar himself. He was amazed how quick he came up with a solution. Now, they all were confident and broke up in their three diversion teams so as to plan how better to surround the dragons and trap them into a fight. Ohnik came up with the best solution and they all agreed, so they broke up their planning discussions and returned to the camp, content, knowing that, even though there were two formidable monsters waiting for them, they had the better plan.

The women had the meal ready which included the freshly caught meat that Ouspa and his men had caught. Ouspa was sure that everyone knew of their fine catch. Soothsay and some women had scoured the hillsides and found a lot of new herbs and other vegetation that was not only suitable to eat, but tasty as well. Even some of the men complimented the cooks on the evening meal. Now, this was a first again and the women were shocked, but happy. That night they all gathered around the ritual fire circle and the families again began chanting and some began pounding boards and make-shift drums. Kibling started his horn music and the children began a dance around the fire. Ohnik. watching with pleasure, spoke to his son, "You know, this is really nice. All the people seem to be genuinely happy. "Yes," Kuballar replied, "The entire colony does seem to be more trusting of each other and of us, but happy?" He thought a moment and added, "Well, maybe just a little."

As the night drew on, little by little, each family took their children and departed into the cave for rest. Now, only the fire keeper and the guards remained awake, watching for danger as the rest slept through the night. This night was peaceful but what would tomorrow bring? Only Bibutsakufascorchum and his arch enemy could relay that message.

It was a nice morning, with the nusea coming up between the clouds. The haze and the morning mist, cast

AGE OF ICE

an eerie glow of purples, blues, and oranges against the mountain and cliffs. While the morning meal was prepared, others, packed carefully, so if they had to make hast along the way, no provisions would be lost. The provision carriers were checked, carefully, to see that all their bundles were tied tightly onto the carrier. The provision carriers were selected for their strength, speed, and endurance. If trouble were to happen, these men or women could outrun and hide the provisions for safe keeping. They were made up mainly of the strongest men who were not good hunters, but some of the strongest, non married women were selected as well.

The plan that Ohnik finalized, was to have the three diversion teams start out ahead of the rest of the colony. Pillas would lead and when he sensed the presence of either beast, they would signal the colony and Comptes would start them on the journey away from the dragon's kingdom. He knew a hidden canyon to the left side of the dragon's domain. It was the same trail that the Adventurers took the first time, to elude Bibutsakufascorchum.

The three teams ventured forth into the dragon's kingdom. They traveled around the scorched section of the woods so they could remain hidden. Half way in, Pillas stopped. "Nay!" he yelled, "I sense danger ahead." Ohnik came up in the ranks and said, "Are you sure and how do you know you are right?" Pillas, quietly replied, "Every time I sense danger, I get a jittery vibration that goes up to my back and into my head. It never fails." "Okay," yelled Ohnik, break off and find a hiding place." Pillas shouted back, "There is a hidden canyon just up ahead, so follow me." They all followed him through a small opening that led to a larger canyon. Once inside and safe, they gathered together to reaffirm their plans and individual tasks.

They all moved out, following Pillas to their destiny with the dragon. The sun had not moved a hands width, when Pillas again motioned them to stop. He

AGE OF ICE

spoke softly now, pointed through the trees at the left and said, "There, about a hundred lengths behind those rock formations, is one of the dragons, which one I do not know." Ohnik, now believed him and said, "We must lay low here and some one must circle around and find the other dragon or our plan will not work." They sat behind the rocks and quietly discussed the problem. Finally Pillas and Philcor volunteered to find the other dragon. Their plan was to find the other dragon and bring back the whereabouts of him and then they all could make some more definite strategy.

They left quietly and the others tried to make no sounds so they wouldn't alert the dragon before them. They sat motionless for about a hand width of the sun, when all of a sudden, the dragon, who up to this point, lay half asleep, put out a roar, shot fire out of one fire port and smoke out of the other. He turned his head towards the colony and moved slowly towards the hidden canyon. In spite of how quiet they were, he had heard their movements somehow and began to rise and make angry sounds in there direction. It was also too late for a diversion team to lure him away. He got up and slowly headed toward the sounds and roaring in dragon language, "No one is going to invade my kingdom and live to tell others."

Pillas's danger sensing devices kicked in at the same time he and Philcor spotted the other dragon. It was no more than 50 lengths from them and Pillas and his father. As his senses recorded the first dragon closing in on Ohnik and the diversion group, he yelled to his father, "No time for any teams to divert the dragon, come, we must make him follow us to Bibutsakufascorchum. I just got a message that that nasty old dragon has spotted our diversion group in the canyon." His father looked at him and asked, "Just the two of us?" Pillas answered, "We have no choice, if we get the other teams, it will too late. We must jump out now and run for that two headed dragon, in hopes that we divert him from

AGE OF ICE

consuming Ohnik and his crew." "Okay, let's do it," was Philcor's reply and with that they began to shout and wave their arms attracting the dragon to them. As they did this the dragon turned and saw them. He got up out of his lair, roared, and spouted fire half way across to where Pillas and Philcor were standing. They began to run and the dragon followed them, down the rocky ledge toward Bibutsakufascorchum. They had a head start and they knew they needed it, for with the dragons huge legs, it could easily out run them. They were at least fifty lengths ahead of him, but after the dragon got his huge body moving, the dragon starting closing in on the gap. Down and down they went toward the two headed dragon. The dragon had gained ground on them and now was only twenty-five paces from them. They hit the flat open and burnt floor closer to Bibutsakufascorchum and now the dragon was only fifteen paces away. It was lucky for them that dragon could not shoot its fire while running or they would now be fried steak for the dragon's meal. The dragon stopped and shot fire at them but they made enough headway to escape the flames. Only some smelly fumes blew there way. But, in the near distance behind them, they saw the grostiks ablaze. As Pillas starting running faster, he yelled to his father, "Run for your life!" But Philcor answered, "Son, you run as fast as you can and save yourself for I am older, let him catch me!" "No Father," was Pillas response, "I sense that we both will make it to Bibutsakufascorchum in time, for he is just a little further ahead of us." "Let's hope so," returned Philcor, and with that, they both put forth extra speed as the dragon stopped a second time to shoot his fire at them. They could feel the heat but the flames did not hit them. The dragon started out again and just as he was about to get close enough to blast them into fries, but there directly in front of them was Bibutsakufascorchum headed for the opening of the canyon. They turned and ran behind a bunch of thickly leafed grostiks. Daggar stopped to see where they went only to find himself standing directly in front of Bibutsakufascorchum.

AGE OF ICE

There was a long moment of silence as both dragons looked surprised at each other's presence. Then, Bibutsakuf stopped, turned and faced the other dragon, "By fire and ashes, if it isn't my old enemy and intruder, Daggar," he said remotely to himself, "but the noises were coming from the left, Daggar came from the right. He pondered this for a moment and continued, "No time for thought, I will take care of that later, now I have an enemy to destroy." He turned and charged Daggar. Daggar didn't see Bibutsakuf coming. He was busying himself with the task of getting rid of those little creatures he was chasing. He could smell them behind that thick clump of grostiks. He was just about to shoot a fiery blast and incinerate them, when, From his left and just behind him, came another stream of fire that hit him on his scaly back, scorching them and searing the flesh underneath. Even though his scales were thick and tough, this hot blast melted through and found its mark in the soft flesh below. The smoke and stench bloomed up into the grostiks and Pillas and Philcor could even smell it as Daggar screamed in agony and pain. The agony and pain was tremendous as he turned and saw Bibutsakuf just five lengths from him. They both looked at each other and hatred glared from their eyes. Quickly, Daggar turned his attention away from the pursuit of his smaller enemies and faced his worst enemy. "Now it is your turn," shouted Daggar, as he gathered all his strength and gave one large blast of fire. It hit Bibutsakuf's right head, straight in the middle. Bibutsakuf screamed in pain with his other head, but the fire had hit its mark and the head was all black and dead. Steaming and smoking, the seared head fell limply to the ground.

Daggar took cover behind a tall pillar and Bibutsakuf retreated to check his wounds. He checked himself over, carefully, and found himself alright, except for his right side, which now was really in pain. "But you now must not falter," he said, reassuring himself, "this is the moment you have been waiting for, it is the moment of your intruder's

AGE OF ICE

death." Bibutsakuf had an advantage over his adversary he knew the territory by heart. He took advantage of this and circled around behind Daggar and before Daggar had a chance to turn, Bibutsakuf blasted him over and over, until his fire juices ran dry. He hit him first, into his head, then his body on one side and then the other. To make sure, he used his last juices to redo his head. The fire came with all its fury and consumed Daggar's head. Having only one head, Daggar didn't have a chance.

BIBUTSAKUFASCORCHUM

AND

DAGGAR

AGE OF ICE

He lurched upwards and twisted sideways in pain and agony. Then he dropped limply to the ground. Bibutsakuf came quickly to his adversary and approached him slowly. Finding him limp and lifeless, he tore into Daggar's body with his claws and teeth, tearing, ripping, and dismembering it with all his fury. He was relentless. He would not quit until his enemy had paid for all the turmoil he had caused Bibutsakufascorchum and most of all, taking half of his own being in the fight.

While Bibutsakuf was maiming and tearing his old dead enemy apart, he did not notice that the three diversion teams had closed in on him. The three teams had caught up to Pillas and Philcor and found them safe. They then surrounded the giant dragon as he kept on gouging, tearing and ripping Daggar apart, still unaware of the three teams.

Joncar's team approached from the front to get his attention. Joncar and two hunters stepped out from behind the rocks and approached Bibutsakuf with their spears drawn. Bibutsakuf stopped his maiming and tearing. He looked suddenly up and there before him were the three Age of Icemen with drawn spears, The dragon took one look and roared in dragon talk, "So there were more intruders after all, just as I had thought. I knew my senses would not deceive me. Now I must do you in as well, you little varmints." Ending his roar, he quickly gathered all the inner gases that he had left and ignited them with his electro nerve endings. Then, he sent a fiery stream of flames, directly at Joncar and the other hunters. Too late to duck, the flames hit them straight on. When the smoke settled, all the bodies were black and seared beyond recognition.

Before Bibutsakuf had a chance to see who else was around, the others attacked. Ohnik,s men attacked from the rear, stabbing cutting, and tearing gashes in between his thick scales and under his soft parts of his back legs. Bibutsakuf raised his front feet up to turn on his attackers, but his back legs

AGE OF ICE

were crippled and he couldn't move. He roared loudly and spit what little fire he had left, but it flew wildly into the rocks. At the same time, Philcor and his men managed to crawl up the rough scales of the dragon by his dead, second head and started chopping and flailing with their sharp stone axes. Philcor managed to scale up the good head and thrust his axe, directly into Bibutsakuf's right good eye. His best trained axe hunter had scaled up the other side and hit his left eye. Bloody liquids started gushing out of both eyes and Philcor and his cohort had to duck back behind his head to avoid the slimy river that flowed from his, now, blinded eyes. Bibutsakufascorchum roared and screamed in terror. He reared up and shook his head, trying to throw his assailants off, but the hunters were pros at killing big beasts and the dragon had met his match. They had stuck their spears and axes deep into his hide and used them to hang on as he shook and twisted to no avail.

Try as he may, Bibutsakufascorchum could not get rid of his attackers. To make it even worse, the third party had crawled under his soft belly and neck and chopped furiously at all the soft spots. Three men had managed to open a gapping hole in his neck. There they found his jugular vein and severed it. The blood gushed in spurts like a flowing red river. His life line was slowly diminishing as the blood flowed helplessly onto the rocks below. In his last desperate attempt, Bibutsakufascorchum shot one more fiery spurt helplessly into the rocks. He reared up as high as his crippled body would let him, roared one more loud agonizing scream and fell thunderously to the ground. All the men on him were well trained, sensing his fall, they jumped safely to the ground below.

They all stood there a long time before the dragon as he quivered and shook in his dying moments. It was almost pitiful to see such a splendid beast die like this but it was either the dragon or the colony and they knew which they had to choose. When

AGE OF ICE

Bibutsakufascorchum finally stopped moving Ohnik, Philcor, and a few other hunters went gingerly up to his body. They examined it and poked at it to make sure it was dead. Pillas came up and assured them that all danger signs had ceased.

They left the dragon's body and went sadly over to their dead, charred comrades. They lay in a pile of smoldering ashes. They took count and only Joncar and two of his men were hit and killed. The rest of the men all seemed alright, except for some cuts and bruises. Ohnik spoke to all of them, "Men, we have all faced death in the hunt before. Joncar was old and has had many good hunts to take with him. The other men are heroes as is our beloved Joncar. Let us bury them under the rocks where they died. We will then give tribute and be on our way." They built a type of rock memorial to mark the graves and headed off to find the hidden canyon.

CHAPTER EIGHT: THE COLONY SAVED AWAITS THEIR HEROES

Comptes was a good navigator. While the diversion teams had been busy with the two dragons, He led the colony straight to the canyon. It was far enough away that no one even detected their presence. It was hidden well and even Comptes took a moment to find it. There were two tall pillars on each side of a deep dark incline in the middle. The colony followed Comptes down a narrow, dark passage. This turned into a flat creek bed that had a gentle and gradual decline. Eventually the creek opened into a larger river bed. Comptes stopped at it's bank and rested the colony. As they rested, he took some of the men and scouted ahead, to see the present conditions of the river. When they first arrived, at this point, the river was almost dry, but on their return, it was a raging river. They had a very difficult time getting across it. Comptes and his scouts found, to their luck, that no heavy rains had fallen recently, and the river was passable. There were some small rapids, and a few deep pools but most of the river seemed calm and inviting. At least he knew they would have plenty of water for drinking and cooking, for on the Adventurers first trip, there were occasions down here in the warm lands, that they had to hunt for water. They were not used to this, for in the land of ice, there was always an abundance of water.

When they got back the colony packed up and headed down the river bed. It was hard for some of the old people and some children, to make it down this narrow, rocky, and steep incline, but once down, it flattened out and opened to a wide and gentle decline. Comptes led the colony down the same path they had scouted, earlier. It was not all flat and smooth. Occasionally, they came to a rocky steep ridge that the river had cut, as it flowed down more forcefully. At the bottom of each ridge, there

AGE OF ICE

was a pool of water that would be six to ten paces deep. In some places, it was even difficult to find enough boulders along the edges for all the colony members to scale by. After they all got through successfully, Comptes decided that they all deserved a rewarding rest and refreshments. As they stopped and rested, it also became a blessing for them, for it was here that the colony could load up with cool, fresh water. They were starting to find it a task to locate enough water for all their needs. When there was water available, it wasn't always where they camped and hauling enough for drinking and cooking, was out of the question. They were not used to searching for water for up in Feriandimal, they had ice and water everywhere. Comptes had gone out of his way and warned all the colony, but some did not listen and ran short and tried to beg or steal from others. This led to some small troubles that soon waned when all learned to heed Comptes's warnings. While they were relaxing, some of the colony, including Comptes, noticed, what looked like lightning and sounds of thunder as well. Some asked Comptes if there was lightning and thunder here when there were no clouds, but Comptes told them that it was the fight of the dragon against the three diversion groups. "We will learn, soon, what results they had with that dragon," he reported to them. "In the meantime do not worry, for those men have many years of experience fighting big beasts, and even Bibutsakufascorchum, is not smart enough to outwit all those brave fighters." They all seemed satisfied with his report. Kibling took Comptes aside and asked, "I know your trying to quell the colony, but don't you think, a beast of that size, who has maintained a kingdom for who knows for how long, could even do damage to many of our brave fighters?" Comptes looked him straight in the eye and said, "I will not try to fool you, for you have seen him with your own eyes. Yes there is a good chance that some will be hurt and even killed, but I know our plan will work."

The noises and light flashes stopped and they

AGE OF ICE

packed up and followed Comptes down the river bed. They journeyed down, down, and down. Soon they reached the lower and warmer section of the mountain. There was a large, mesa-like area, where there were large high flying black creatures circling overhead. It was here that Kibling showed Soothsay all the abundance of herbs and eatable plants. Comptes, as well took time out to show all the people the fruit plants and told them only to eat the red ones. Just a little further up, Comptes led them to a large cave. In front there was a large opening in the canyon, where the three rivers came together. It was awesome to look at and many of the colony members started their uuhs and aahs, looking at the splendor of this sight. There were even more spectacular sights, for they were used to only short scraggly grostiks, but now before them, were tall, slender grostiks with great colorful plumes spreading out over their tops. Some of the plants had many different colorful blumens and some had round things that Comptes called, plumefrus.

The sun had only moved nine hands around the sky. It would usually be too early to stop for the night, but Comptes got all the family leaders together and said, "This was the only suitable camping area, large enough for the colony, and we do not want to journey too far ahead of the diversion teams. I'm sure all of you are eager to find out the results of their fight with the dragon." They talked it over and all agreed that this was a choice for all. The colony went about their regular tasks, while Comptes sent some of the guards back to the hidden canyon opening to guide the diversion teams down to this cave.

Without Comptes to guide them, they took longer than they wanted. They jig-jagged back and forth, sometimes coming back to their original trail. Frustrated, Ohnik remarked, "It is times like this that you appreciate Comptes and his uncanny insights into our journey." "You are so right," replied Pillas, "when he led us on our adventure and

AGE OF ICE

back, we were always amazed as to how he could always find the right direction and trail. From here to our Promised Land and back, we depended on him entirely."

Finally, they reached the canyon and found two of the rear guards, waiting for them. They all were glad to see each other. Philcor was even more surprised and asked, "How come you are here waiting for us?" One of the two guards replied, "Well, Comptes insisted that they back track and wait for you to arrive. The trail down to the colony is tricky to follow, so he wanted to make sure you had a guide." "That was really nice of him for thinking of us," replied Philcor, "what say we up and follow these two fine men, back to the colony. "It sounds good to me," replied Ohnik. The two guards, quickly, took the three diversion teams down the steep and winding trail to meet the colony.

The men in the diversion teams were amazed at the walls of the canyon. The walls were almost a 90° vertical and very high. As they descended, they noticed a sudden change in the scenery. The floor was now mostly a dry river bed. One could see that, years ago, the abundance of rushing water had cut away the soft rock, leaving tall black pillars, like stoic guards on watch.

The icemen made their way down the canyon and were in awe at the changes and the beauty of the canyon. Journeying further down the canyon they looked up and saw, way high up, above the pillars, strange creatures that had wings that flopped up and down, as they glided around the pillars. They all stopped and admired these creatures, pointing to them, and wondered what they were. After awhile of staring, they decided that these creatures were not coming down, so they continued on their way.

They wound their way down the river bed and found another unusual sight. There were large green, bushy grostiks all over the canyon. Some had

AGE OF ICE

plumefrus and others were decorated with blumens. They had never seen this before. In Feriandimal, in the ice fields, only little twiggy plants grew out of the ice and rocks. They only had small dark leaves. Here, there were plants in abundance and more and more of them as they went along. They had round green and red spheres on them that fascinated the icemen. They stopped and Ohnik picked a green one and was about to eat it , when Pillas yelled, "No, Ohnik, not the green ones, eat the red ones!" Knowing Pillas's sensing devices, he quickly dropped the green one and picked a red one, placing it in his mouth. He began chewing, slowly at first, but as the flavors set in, he chewed rapidly and thrust more and more in his mouth. Soon, Pillas cautioned him again, Ohnik, if I were you, I wouldn't eat so many. I know how delicious they taste, but you are not used to them and they may make you sick." The other ate some as well, but followed Pillas's advice.

"Come," said one of the guards, "we must hurry or we will not catch the colony till dark." "You are right," said Ohnik, we got caught up in all this new and different scene, that we lost track of time." They all packed up and headed down the trail, following the two guards. The guards led the diversion teams further down and closer to the colony's camp. It was the same river bed as Comptes led the colony. As they descended and their surroundings changed, they also were amazed and pleased, with all the new surprises. As they rounded each bend there was a new surprise. They made their way down past the same ridges, pools and then, as they turned the last bend, there was the cave, the large expanse and the colony. At the same time the guards saw the colony, Kibling blew his goula horn, to announce the diversion groups' arrival. Some of the colony members, hearing the horn, ran out to meet the diversion groups, while some of the diversion group was so anxious, that they broke ranks and dashed for their loved ones.

HERO'S WELCOME

CHAPTER NINE: THE HEROES WELCOME & A SON'S REPLY

There was joy and rejoicing in the colony. The news of the dragon killing and the return of so many that were safe, led most colony members to rejoice, but when Ohnik told Kibling of the tragic news of his father, there was an immediate silence. All watched, as Kibling, immediately, grabbed his son Arteson and ran.

As soon as he was out of sight and he knew he wouldn't be heard, he ran briskly deep into the cave, screaming and crying shouts of anger as they retreated. He ran with his son, from one tunnel to another, deeper and deeper he went in his remorse. Finally, he controlled his passions and his intellect kicked in. Now, he began to search for a suitable area to carve his memorial to his father. Arteson was the first to locate a suitable sight that had enough light from an overhead hole in the rough of the cave.

Kibling hugged his son and said, "You are extra special in my life. Now that my father is gone, you are my joy and care. You have proven your worth and good by this and many other challenges. Now, let us make a memorial to your grandfather's heroic deeds." With those words, he picked out a suitable area on the wall and assigned one part for Arteson and one part for his tribute. He found two sharp, jagged rocks and fine honed them for their chisels. He gave one chisel to his son and said, "You carve a memory of your grandfather's hunt and I will carve the dragon and my father, where he stood firm for the colony, as the dragon consumed him."

They had no paint with them or places they could make it, so the memorial had to be carved. It did not diminish the quality and effort of their work. They both labored hard and long on their work. Each interpreting his own idea of a memorial. Little did

AGE OF ICE

they realize, that in centuries beyond, Trolldar would take the Earth artisans and Etudadorma scholars back and uncover this truly magnificent memorial, a tribute to a father, and a grandfather. in centuries to come and beyond, it would become a monumental landmark.

While Kibling and Arteson were busy paying homage to Joncar, the rest of the colony was celebrating their good fortune. The Women prepared a special feast. They roasted part of the dragon's flesh that the diversion team had brought back with them, which always was a ritual tribute to a victorious hunt. The women also prepared a real special, added menu. They had found, with Soothsay's help, special herbs, fruit, nuts and berries, that later, Comptes and Soothsay, had given special names.

When Kibling and Arteson finished their memorial and returned to the festivities that were going on, they did not miss out of much of the stories of the killing of the two dragons. The stories went on into the night and multiplied in their glories, as each hero would try to make his story better. Ohnik probably had the most accurate story as he related it around the ritual fire circle that night. He began by saying, "When I saw the dragon shoot fire at Joncar and his men, I and my men, attacked his back legs. With all our past experience and with perfect forceful maneuvers, we were able to slash, jab, and cut away all the working parts of his back legs so that he was unable to move them." The day was waning, but most of the colony sat around the ritual fire circle, listening intently to Ohnik's story. When he was through, they chanted and shouted the words of victory. Philcor got excited to the crowds enthusiasm and started his own story, as soon as Ohnik finished., "I tell you that dragon was a fearful sight to behold. He stood ten lengths of our people high and both his heads could spurt out fire many paces away, but when we saw Ohnik and his men attack the dragons front legs, we quickly attacked the dragon's head and neck. With my new and

AGE OF ICE

advanced axes, we were able to slice and chop big holes in his head and puncture both his eyes. You should have seen the gushing of fluids and blood flow out of him and all the while, he screamed, shook, and twisted, frantically in pain. We were able to hang on because we wedged our feet deep into his large scales. While we were doing this, my other men chopped a whole in his soft underside of his neck. They then found his main blood vessels and cut them in two. Boy, the blood flowed like a river until he got too weak and fell dead. Again, the crowd chanted and shouted the words of victory and celebrated the diversion teams great feats.

Soon they became quiet when they realized that the third team leader was not here to tell his story. Kibling and Arteson had just returned, and sensing the awkwardness of the situation, he stepped up and took his father's place and began to speak, "I was not there, as you all know, but my father's loyal fighters, the ones that survived, have filled me in on all the details of their experiences. My father, Joncar, seeing what had to be done to get the dragon down, drew attention to himself and his team, thereby putting himself in harms way. He did this to save the rest of us, knowing full well that this could cost him and his men, their lives. He and his men stepped forward in the line of the dragon's fire so that the other teams would have time to chop that beast to his demise. I therefore honor my father and let us not forget my father's heroic fighters who also gave up their lives for us."

There was silence among the crowd as Kibling finished. It was sad to see one of their leaders die, soon, the crowd again broke out in a victory chant which grew and soon, they were all dancing and shouting around the ritual fire circle. This went on into the night and until many stumbled, exhausted to bed. Both Ohnik and Philcor could not sleep, including many of their fighters. The dramatic events of the day were too much for sleep to

AGE OF ICE

take it's toll. All the fury of battling the two dragons, plus these little Age of Icemen, challenging those big beasts, kept racing through their minds. It was the largest and the fiercest beast that they had ever encountered, and as small as they were, they still managed to kill the monster. These thoughts kept going over and over in their minds. Ohnik turned his thoughts and wondered if they would have been this successful, if it weren't for their encounter with the Glowing Ball of Knowledge. Philcor, on the other hand, felt quite different. He accepted in his own mind that the development of his advanced axe, plus the training of his men to a skill level, played a very important part in the victory.

But their were two others who could not sleep. Kibling and Arteson tried to imagine the great heroism of Joncar. What it would be like to get a full force of the dragons fire in your face. Was he able, now to hear us and be pleased with our celebration and memorial of him. Slowly they too fell sound asleep. The only sounds remaining, was the crackle of the fire and the wind blowing in through the leaves of the grostiks.

The night passed quickly. The nooma reflect had just set and the guards noted the breaking light of the new born day. Already, many of the older men were up and attending the fires. The women too were already busy with the morning meal. Ohnik arose and went looking for Kibling. He was more than curious about what kind of a tribute, Kibling and Arteson had left in memory of Joncar. He found him talking to Kuballar. He came up to them and asked, "Would you please tell me, for I am very curious about what you have made their in this cave?" Kibling replied, "Why yes, I'd be glad to, in fact, I was just telling your son all about it." He went on and explained every detail that he and Arteson had done. Ohnik then said, Now, I am really dying to see this think that the two of you have made. Go get your son and Kuballar and I will find torches

AGE OF ICE

for us and prepare them so we can all a look at your masterpiece."

Kibling led them back into the area where the carving was located. He stopped and remarked, I am pleased to show you our work, but after the last one I did, I'm not too anxious to have the others see it. You remember all the murmuring and questions many had, well, I really am not up to going through that right now." But Father," Arteson replied, "I am proud of what we have done and I would like to show everybody our work." Ohnik responded quickly, "No, Arteson, your father is right. It is better to keep it a memorial just for the few of us who understand. We have enough murmuring and bickering without adding a new issue." They finally all agreed and Kibling led them to the carving.

Ohnik and Kuballar looked intently at the two carvings. They walked back and forth, observing every chisel mark they made. They both asked some questions as to why this or that was done the way it was. When both were filled with the mesmerizing affect it had on them, they went over to the outer edge of the room. There they bowed down on the floor and gave reverence. There was a long period of silence and both, Kibling and Arteson did not know what to do or say. Finally, Ohnik and Kuballar got up. hugged them and Ohnik replied, "Both of you are filled with magic. This carving is just as we experienced it on the battle field. You have special powers that we can surely use in the new land."

Kibling was very pleased with Ohnik's response. Arteson looked on and smiled, knowing how important this was coming from the leader of the colony, who now was honoring his father, and now he said to himself, he is even giving tribute to me," and in his eyes, this was extra special.

Kuballar too gave them praise but it was taken more, as a close friendship, than a serene accolade such as his father had done.

A SON'S MEMORIAL

THE AGE OF ICE

CLOSE UP MAP OF JOURNEY'S CENTRAL TRAIL

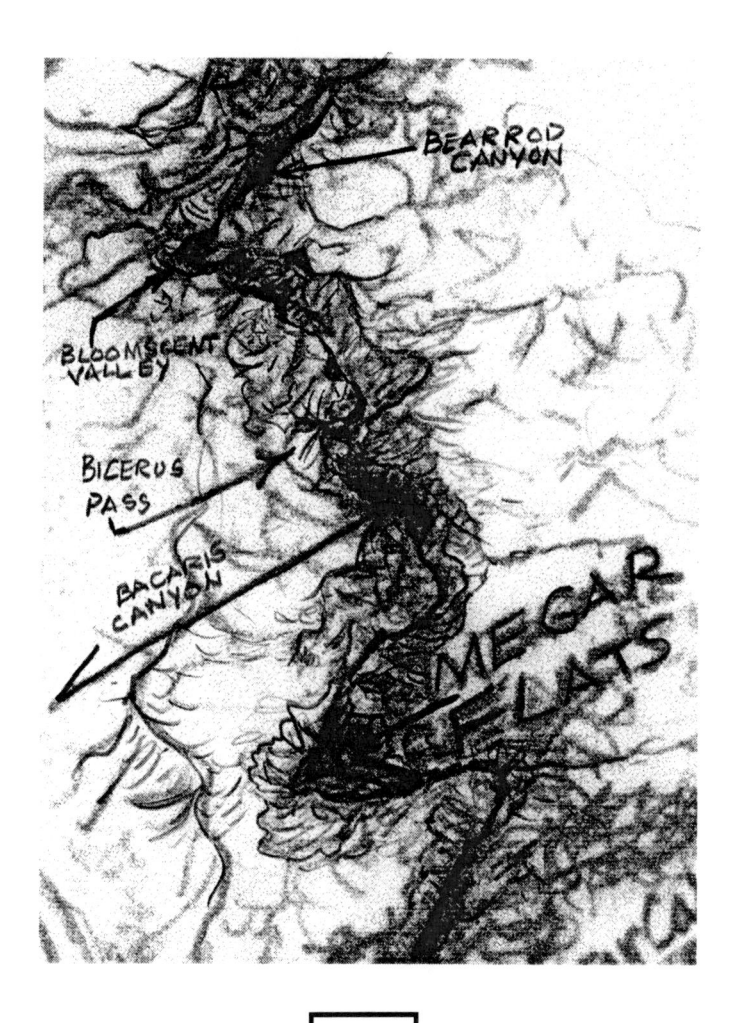

Labels on map: BEARROD CANYON, BLOOMSCENT VALLEY, BICERUS PASS, BACARIS CANYON, MEGAR FLATS

95 MAP

CHAPTER TEN:
WARMTH, SWEAT, & THE RUBALANGERS

When they returned to the opening of the cave, Comptes was already giving orders to the leaders. Immediately, they realized that they had spent too much time in the cave and quickly joined the team leaders in organizing the colony for the days hike. Kuballar gathered his Adventures for a last minute update and soon, they were off again, treading a new and ever changing environment into no mans land. The sun had moved only two hands by the time Comptes was moving the colony down the trail. The Adventurers and the head leaders took the same positions except Kibling. With the death of his father, he now became Joncar's replacement as a hunter and colony trail leader as well as maintaining his head responsibilities as an Adventurer. He had to adjust to his new role, but as a creative person, his flexibility helped him to adapt quickly. As a front team, Kuballar and Comptes not only made a good team to direct all the others, but they had time together to make future plans as to how to set up the kingdom when they arrived at their new home.

They descended gradually without any interruptions from outside intruders. As they descended, the land and plants began taking on different shapes. With the ice and black rocky ridges behind them, the land gave way to a smoother surface. The warmer climate, plus, the run off from the higher mountain ridges made the soil rich and thicker, this allowed for a greater abundance and varieties of plant life. As they passed by some low and flat areas, they were amazed at how large and high some of the grostiks were getting. In our eyes, it would have looked like a rain forest.

Ohnik sent word to Comptes that they needed a rest. Comptes found a nice open, flat area and stopped. Ohnik also was anxious to talk to Comptes about how

AGE OF ICE

much he enjoyed the beauty and how warm it was getting. As soon as they stopped, he went up the column to the front where Comptes was just sitting down on a rock and relaxing. He saw Ohnik coming and said, "Hey, Ohnik, over here! Come sit down and let us talk a spell." That was just what Ohnik wanted to hear. It was as though Comptes was reading his mind. He came over, sat down, and said, "Why that is why I came up here so quickly. I want to tell you how excited I am over the changes of the land. This is really more than I imagined!" Comptes looked at him and smiled, saying, "This is only the beginning of awesome beauty and rich lands." Ohnik smiled back in acceptance of his statement and added, "There is one other situation I had not thought of. The weather is getting warmer and warmer. Many of the people are really starting to sweat." Comptes looked down the rows of people and saw that many were really sweating, and said, "We must make a plan now for shedding clothes. The Age of Icemen do not know of such a thing. It will get cold as the nusea lowers, so they must be prepared to bundle up again." They discussed this problem with the other leader and set up an instructional policy for all to go by. The plan they decided on, was of gradually take off the layers of fur and tie them to their hips. When the weather got colder, they could put on the layers as needed. While they were resting and having refreshments, the family leaders went to everybody and gave them the new information.

It was just one hand past the high nusea when they left again. They had many lengths ahead of them before they could camp. It was almost a funny sight to see. Everyone had layers of furs, dangling on their sides and bouncing up and down as they walked down the trail. Some men even bared their hairy arms, something they had never done outside before. Down, down, and down they went, and it got warmer and warmer as they descended. Ohnik, talking to one of his men said, "You know, I believe the weather out there feels the same as my skin does in here,

AGE OF ICE

and he pointed to his chest. They continued on an enjoyable afternoon and Comptes found the next camp site right on schedule.

The camp was a large open area, devoid of tree. It did not have any caves, but there were plenty of large over hangs to camp under. The families went about their usual routine and set up their camp for the night. It was just one day away from the valley floor and the Adventurers wanted to make plans for the leaders for they knew there were many things still to be resolved, in order to get down to the valley floor. They called a meeting, while the others prepared the meal and lodging.

Comptes and Kuballar spoke for the Adventurers. Comptes addressed the leaders first, "My fellow colony leaders, we have journeyed long and had some dangerous experiences. We came through with courage and skill. We have since left the ice fields of our home and are past Mount Morgan, where we battled the dragon and defeated him. You are now about to journey down the last part of the mountain. You then will go through Bearrod Canyon and down into Bloomscent Valley. As you experienced, particularly today, it is getting warmer. Soon it will be even warmer and you may not need furs at all and when you get to the valley, there will be beauty beyond belief. You will smell fragrances of great pleasure, but, again, I must warn you, not all will be this pleasant. When you pass through the valley, you will enter Tucksay Narrows where rubalangers are in abundance in the sides of the canyon walls. They are in the crevices of rocks and when you pass, they strike out at you, biting and sucking your blood. So if you aren't diligent, many will wrap around you and suck so much blood from you, that you will become weak. There are as many as all the hands of the colony can count. They strike you from the sides, the top and behind you. I am not telling you this to discourage you, only to caution you, so you may be well prepared."

AGE OF ICE

There started that same mumbling and whispering again when trouble is announced. Ohnik, wanting to cut it off before it started to get out of hand, raised his voice and asked, "How did you Adventurers get through alive?" Comptes was quick to reply, "They are not big enough to kill you, they only irritate but with many attacks, they can make you sick. When we went through the first time, we retreated when they struck at us and we talked it over first. Kuballar came up with the solution. We put all our furs on and ran through as fast as we could. It was hot and a few still got us but we made it there and back." Kuballar then got up and spoke,, "Yes, friends, we will prevail, so don't worry. If we all dress so only our faces show, we will be alright. I know it will be hot, but that's better than bites from those nasty rubalangers.

The gathered leaders looked at one another and started to whisper and discuss it amongst themselves. Then, Kuballar quickly intervened and said, "Leaders, hunters, and fellow friends, I know this sounds bad, but it isn't as bad as it sounds. We will be here in camp another day and we can make plans to come up with a better solution. We have before and I am confident that we will now." He was going to continue and tell them about the evil winged armaflorvias in the Megan Flats, but looking into their worried faces, he thought it wiser to wait till they got through the Tucksay Narrows and the rubalanger problem first.

They all went back to camp somewhat satisfied and Kuballar talked to his father and asked that they have a high level conference between the Adventurers and the other top leaders. Ohnik consented and said he would arrange it. As he left to find the others, Kuballar contacted his Adventurers and told them of his plans. They met and discussed the problem all afternoon but no one seemed to come up with a solution that was failsafe. After wrangling to almost exhaustion, they decided to postpone it and enjoy the evening meal.

AGE OF ICE

It was a joy to behold. As they came into camp, there were the camp the cooks preparing the fresh meat that some of the hunters had killed. The prey here was plentiful and easy hunting. Some of the younger women and older men, went out into the woods and found fresh fruit, nuts and berries. The evening meal was extra special and some of the men even commented to the cooks how good it was. This was another first in the life of the Age of Icemen After they had finished some of the men started blowing their horns and others found hollow logs and began beating on them. Arteson had designed a reed that sounded almost like a flute and he joined in. Kibling hearing the sounds that was almost musical, got his goula and joined them as well. They sounded wild and out of tune but it didn't matter, for in the joy and excitement of the moment, the young ones got up and danced around the fire, singing and shouting as they danced. Soon the hunters and older men began some rhythmical chanting sounds. Kibling and Arteson's sensitivities got the best of them and they went outside . There they got their composer and Arteson stretched a skin, tightly over a hollow log and found some good sturdy sticks and went back in. He then began to beat a rhythm and his father followed it with his horn. Soon all caught on and the cave, there was a sound that seemed like music. They sang, chanted and danced into the night, until exhaustion overcame them, and each slipped quietly off to dream of a dawning of a new age. Even the night watch seemed to enjoy the warm night air and the fragrant aroma coming up from the valley below.

The nusea was just rising and giving its eerie colorful glow, as it rose above the mountains. Ohnik, Philcor, and Jealon left camp for a rendezvous meeting with their sons. The unfinished business of the day before, lay heavy on all their minds. All of them wanted a solution to the rubalangers dilemma. The three men found their sons behind the far ledge that overlooked the valley below. When they arrived, the four Adventurers were already in deep discussion and Jealon suddenly remarked to them, "I suppose you already have the problem solved?" Comptes quickly replied, "No, Father, we are still as lost for a solution as we were last night." They went back and forth all morning and finally, decided to break for the midday meal.

Their discussions went on and on and got them nowhere so Kuballar and Comptes decided to stay and see if they couldn't find a solution by themselves. As they stood there talking, Kuballar stared at where the narrows started and saw a strange rock formation. It was shaped in such a way that he visualized it as an axe striking the tree behind it. He burst out a cry, "That's it!" Comptes, being surprised by his sudden shout, asked, "What's it? I see nothing." Kuballar explained, pointing to the rock, "That rock there, hitting that grostik." then, Comptes was even more confused and asked, "I see it but what does that prove?" "My good friend," said Kuballar, "it is showing me a sign. The answer is simple, we take the smallest young men and put animal heads on them. When the rubalangers strike at them, we will place Philcor and his trained axe hunters directly behind them and they will quickly chop them into pieces. By sending six to eight youth in rows and axe hunter behind, we should be able to clear the canyon of most of those pesky worms.

Comptes just looked at him astounded. Finally he said, "Great, you've done it again. Just how do you do this, I mean, keep coming up with all the right answers at the right time?" Kuballar looked back at him and replied, "I really don't know! I guess the only answer I can come up with is the touching of the Glowing Ball of Knowledge. After all, Comptes, you have done some pretty spectacular things yourself, as the other Adventurers." "Well, I guess you're right, so let's go back to the others and tell them of this great solution, replied Comptes.

They still were eating when they returned so they

AGE OF ICE

said nothing, preferring to feast down first. After the meal the leaders all met and continued the debate. Comptes asked Kuballar, quietly, "Should we tell them?" "No," Kuballar replied, "let's wait until the right moment comes along in this discussion." So on the leaders went, arguing and debating every different proposal, but to no avail. Then, it happened, two leaders got mad at each other, over some silly argument. One grabbed his spear and the other his knife. Kuballar, sensing the trauma, stepped in between them and said, "Men, Killers of beasts, my good friends, let us not get excited over some trivial matter. Please, calm yourselves and listen to me, for I have important news." They dropped their weapons and the whole group stopped and looked intently at Kuballar. Kuballar stepped up to the circle of men and spoke, "Comptes and I have spent time after you left for the high nusea meal. We discussed the problem thoroughly and have come up with a good workable solution, that I think, you will agree to. Here is what we planned. First, we must find the smallest young men and fit them with the animal heads we have stored. Second, we organize an equal number of axe hunters to follow close behind them. The plan is this, the young men with animal heads will file through the canyon about six to eight in number. The axe hunters will follow close behind. When the worms attach the young ones heads, the hunters will use their axes to slice them in to pieces. With enough groups, we should be able to wipe out most of those nasty worms, thereby giving the rest of us, very little discomfort."

The leaders looked astonished. They hardly expected these two young men two come up with a solution so fast that they have debated for days. Then one, two, and finally all, started shouting, "We have greatness! We have magic! Let us go forth! Let us go forth!" Ohnik stepped forward and spoke, "Hunters and fellow Age of Icemen, you have now witnessed greatness, so let us now go forward and not ever doubt them again. We will now return to

AGE OF ICE

camp and start a new era of trust and companionship." The group now began to chant in unison, "Butah Mon go! Butah Mon go!" After the celebration and joy, they all returned to camp. The late afternoon and evening went as usual, waiting for the morning, to bring them new adventures.

The next morning was not a usual morning. Every leader and participant checked out all the equipment and procedures, to make sure everything would go as planned. Once they were sure, they were off, down the trail to a destiny of success or utter failure at the slashing and tearing of the vicious worms. There were no surprises down the first part of the trail. The colony worked their way down the mountain pass, toward Bloomscent Valley. They journeyed a few miles through the last mountain trail. Here, they came out to a small valley, filled with flowers, trees, and bushes, that left off scents and fragrances, filled them with ecstasy.

They all suddenly stopped and took in these sudden surprises that was almost overwhelming to them. Philcor asked Kuballar, "Is this where the worms are supposed to attack us?" "Oh no," responded Kuballar, "this is the pleasant surprise I was waiting to show all of you before the agony of the worms. It is an ecstasy of wonders. Come, let us bath ourselves in this luxury."

Bloomscent Valley is a small valley, nestled in the center and surrounded on all sides by mountains, except for the canyon and narrows on each end. The mountains protected it from severe storms and provided the valley with an abundance of rain. The entire valley lay in bloom, and at the same time there was fruit, nuts and berries that lay everywhere, just for the picking. The people in the colony couldn't believe their eyes. They picked and ate till they were full and then picked those things that could be stored. Others, just walked around, taking in the beauty and aroma of the plants. Kuballar looked up at the nusea above him.

AGE OF ICE

It was one hand to the nusea up over and he yelled back to all the family leaders, "I know this is great and you probably don't want to leave just yet, but if we are to get through Tucksay Narrows in day light, we must leave now."

Comptes led them around the right side of the valley. They took in the splendor and fragrance, all through the entire valley, as they journeyed toward the narrows. But soon, the beauty of the valley left them. The land turned rough and rocky. As they moved forward, they entered a narrow and rocky trail. The sides loomed up high over their heads.
It seemed dark and foreboding as they started their journey into it. Soon, Comptes saw the trail ahead become even more narrow. It was the beginning of Tucksay Narrows. He stopped the colony and gathered all the leaders together. "This is the start of Tucksay Narrows," he reported to them, Let us go over our procedure, one more time, then we will gird the youth with heads, position the axe hunters behind them, and line the colony in the correct order. It took over a hand width of the sun before all was ready. Comptes gave them instructions to wait for him to give the signal, before entering the narrows.

It was well into the afternoon when Comptes gave the signal. The first leaders moved their young men and axe hunters into the narrows. They moved cautiously and slow. At first, they encountered nothing unusual, but as they rounded the first bend in the narrows, the worms attacked. First one struck an animal head, worn by the young men, then two, soon hundreds of the rubalangers attacked. They struck from both side walls of the narrows. It seemed overwhelming at first, but when the axe hunters went into action, chopping and slicing the worms in a precise timed order that as they had practiced, the battle turned in favor of the Age of Icemen. Those that they had struck only in half lay squirming and wiggling on the ground, trying to escape and grow their bodies again, but the axe

AGE OF ICE

hunters were quick to see them and chopped them till they lay quiet and quite dead. There was one bad effect that they didn't count on. The axe hunters didn't get all the worms. Some managed to slither back in their holes and attacked later. The worms hit the axe hunter groups from the rear and even, still later, the women and children in the rear of the colony. This proved to be not too serious, for everyone was bundled tightly and the worms had little affect. Kuballar and the other leader, guarding the families, took immediate action and warded off most of the worms before they cut to much damage. Comptes finally saw the opening at the end of the narrows and ran for joy into the next valley.

TUCKSAY NARROWS & THE RUBALANGERS

CHAPTER ELEVEN:
THE LAND CLAIMS ITS OWN

They were finally through and free of the those putrid rubalangers. Comptes and the leading defenders waited in the opening of the valley floor for the rest of the colony to get through. They then gathered the colony into a large circle where they checked everybody for bites and various other fatalities. There were no serious injuries, only some minor bites on a few axe hunters, women and children. Soothsay and his aides attended to the bites by rubbing muca bok, an herbal mud they brought from Feriandimal. The Adventurers and their fathers, met, to discuss the next leg of the trip that led them through the Megar Flats where those beasts from the sky live. Kuballar reminded them of the perils, saying, "Don't you remember, it was there that we were attacked by the armaflorvia." "You're right," replied Comptes, "I remember the encounter of those beasts of the sky. There we were, glorying in all our accomplishments of getting through the Tucksay Narrows, climbing the treacherous Bicerus Pass, winding down the perilous Bacaris Canyon, where the rocks and land move and slide, where there are caverns of unknown depths, and without warning, fissures spurted fire high, into the air. We finally reached, what we thought was the land of paradise, when there, from the skies, came those armaflorvia. We were out in the open, unprotected, when three came at us. One hit Kibling dead center, knocking him to the ground and blood gushing from his wounds. If it weren't for Pillas and his knowledge of the axe, he would not be here today. Pillas saw the danger coming and immediately took his axe, hitting the beast directly, as it came at me for a second attack. He had the armaflorvia's head, laying on the ground, with his second blow. The rest saw what happened and flew away. We retreated back to the canyon, where we planned a better route around the edge of Megar Flats that became a safer voyage." "You're sure right about those events," replied Kibling, "if it wasn't for Pillas's quick sensing of danger and his knowledge of the axe, I would be dead like that flying beast, and probably, the rest of you as well." Kuballar interrupted, "Pillas, you are very wise in these matters, what is your judgment on what we should do?" Pillas stood for a moment and thought about what was just said. Then he looked up and said, "Yes, I did sense the danger, and yes, I did use the skills my father taught me, but as to your question, Kuballar, my answer is that we follow the same path, near the mountain and around the wooded edge of Megar Flats. We will have a better chance to protect ourselves in the woods, for the grostiks are tall and dense there, and make a nice cover for us. I already sense danger is ahead of us so every precaution is worth it." Philcor was listening intently and spoke, "I am pleased to hear that my son has made good use of what I taught him, but I would like to know if it is really worth going that far around, when we can go directly through the center?" I know it is a lot further around then through the flats, but remembering those large sky beasts coming at us, and my sensing of danger going ever stronger, I strongly advise that we take the safe route and adhere to my judgment." They all were shocked at his strong command, for this wasn't like the Pillas of old. Kuballar turned to the group and said, "It is obvious that Pillas has grown in his insights and sensitivity, way beyond what he once had, so, we'll follow his suggestion." It is getting late and nooma reflect will soon be on us. We have perilous travel yet ahead of us before we even get to Megar Flats. Let us find a shelter here so we can camp till the next nusea comes up. We have much to plan with our family leaders, so the extra time will be good." They all agreed and Comptes and a crew went out to find a suitable camp.

While they waited, Kuballar and his father started the process of instructing the family leaders for the coming dangers. Oxenya and his son, Ouspa asked

AGE OF ICE

the same antagonizing questions as they did before, but Kuballar and Ohnik were ready for them and retorted back answers they couldn't dispute. Oxenya would eventually accept what he heard, but his son, Ouspa would always go away, grumbling to himself or others that would listen to him. Comptes and crew soon came back and led them to a sheltered overhang. It was in the forest, just at the edge of the mountain wall. There were no caves here but the shelter seemed adequate anyway to all for most were used to worse conditions than these.

The next day's travel through the valley was without incident. They rested at the edge of Bicerus Pass and Comptes gave the leaders further instructions as what to expect climbing this treacherous pass. "Men," he spoke, "this pass is very rocky and rough. There are many loose boulders that could fall on us. Keep a close vigil and try not to jar any rocks loose. Also, keep your ear tuned to Pillas, for if he senses danger, he will warn you ahead of time so you can take cover.

After all the leaders felt satisfied, Comptes led them into the Bicerus Pass. Pillas, still feeling danger, positioned himself up front with Comptes. The other Adventurers spread out between the columns of people. Everything went well until they got to the turn at the last left ridge that led them to the top of the pass. All of a sudden, without any warning, Pillas got a great sensing of danger that flowed through his body. He turned and shouted the warning signal. It was too late, even for his quick sensing. The steady tramping of feet caused a vibration in the rock formation. This caused the upper rocks and boulders to loose their footing. Slowly one by one, the wedged in rocks began to slide and they came crashing down on the colony. The rocks, dust, and boulders caused an unbelievable amount of devastation, but if it wasn't for Pillas's quick actions, many more would have fallen under the rock slide.

AGE OF ICE

The leaders blew their horns, signaling danger and all the colony came running. Kibling and Pillas was first on the scene. It was horrible. There were tons of rock on the second brigade of the colony. This was Comptes's group. They all were frightened that they would find their leader crushed to death. Soon, all the colony caught up and saw what had happened. Pandemonium set in. Some began screaming in anguish, believing their loved ones trapped below tons of rock. Others yelling, shouting, and milling about, getting into the real rescuers way. Kuballar and Ohnik appeared and calmed the crowd. They got the leaders to move the colony back so the rescuers could work.

Pillas, this time got a good sensing message that ran through his body. He shouted out, "Men, grab your axes, spears, knives and hands and let's dig down here," he pointed to the left of him. "Comptes and some other members of his brigade are still alive and trapped in a hole beneath those rocks." The men immediately grabbed what they had and started digging and throwing off the larger boulders. It was amazing to see two men pick up a five hundred pound boulder and cast it down the canyon. Carefully they dug, trying not to upset the delicate balance of rocks above their comrades. Finally they reached one and he was alright except for some cuts and bruises. They kept digging for they heard voices crying out below. Soon, all were rescued, including, Comptes, who immediately made sure all his brigade was safe. All hugged and shouted for joy over their victory.

When the joy and celebration had ended, some of the colony started to ask where their loved ones were. Pillas bowed his head and sadly announced, "I am terribly sorry to announce that my sensors have told me that all the others have fallen beneath the rocks and are dead. We must, therefore, dig them up and give them proper farewell.

The leaders questioned Pillas's request and asked

AGE OF ICE

for a conference. After much discussion, the group decided that this was the best choice. Even though they were not used to giving farewells to their fellow hunters, because so many die in the hunt and they are accustomed to accept death as a way of life, none the less, it seemed more and more, that the Glowing Ball of Knowledge was influencing all of the Age of Icemen. Its influence, through those who had touched it, was moving them all up the scale of learning and social orders. This influx of learning had led the colony on a path of humanism, so advanced, that even Ohnik and the others who had contact with the ball, could not comprehend all that was changing in their society, yet here they were, laying to rest their loved ones and feeling good about it.

When all the ceremonies were over, Soothsay, double-checked those with cuts and bruises. He administered more salves, herbs. and wrapped the deeper wounds. it was late afternoon by the time they finished.

Ohnik, Philcor, and Jealon, met with the Adventurers. Jealon spoke to them about his concerns for the welfare of the people, "Kuballar, my son was almost killed. The people are really upset right now over what has just happened. Some are still grieving their loved ones. I look in the sky and see the nusea dropping lower in the sky. We must find a place soon to camp and recuperate. is there a place close by?" Kuballar put his hand on Jealon's shoulder and said gently, "I too feel sad for our losses but I am joyous that your son is still with us, and yes, there is a camping sight suitable for us just a short distance up this narrow but rocky trail. We will be at the top of the pass and you will see a large open, flat area. Behind it there is a small cave. We can fit the women and children into the cave and the rest of us can stand guard or rest in the sheltered opening." Is there any perilous beasts roaming up there? If so, I will form an outer double watch of axe hunters to be on the safe side." "No, as I recall, there isn't any animals at all up there," replied Kuballar. I think it is too rocky and baren for them, but even so, I think your idea of a second guard of axe hunters is a good safe guard anyway." "It is good," replied Ohnik, "we will follow you to the Bicerus Pass. I think it is a good idea that we camp there for two or three days. It will give us time to regain our strength and reassure our members of the joy they will receive when they reach the Promised Land."

The trail was only two farthets to the summit. Even though the path was very rough and rocky, there were no other casualties. When the colony arrived at the summit, the sun had not set high up on this peak. As Kuballar had said, there was a great expanse with many overhanging ledges and a small cave in the middle. It was surrounded on three sides with jagged boulders, but being this high up, they could see in all directions. On one side, there was a huge and deep abyss that looked like it had no bottom. In the middle was a high flat cliff that extended high into the sky. It had many large overhanging shelters and a small cave, just as Kuballar had told them.

The entire colony found the top and rested as the leaders conferred. Kuballar gathered the family leaders to one side and said, "Men, There is an adequate cave in the middle of this high cliff. It is not big enough so that you can separate by families, however, you are used to adapting to travel adjustments as needed. So, I urge you to get each of your families to accept this arrangement and then we will organize the women and children in the cave and the men for outside watches and resting."

The family leaders quickly huddled the families together and explained the circumstances that existed. After explaining the plan, they came to Kuballar for the final organization. It went smoothly and the women and children even enjoyed their stay

AGE OF ICE

together. There was still room for some elderly men and those injured more severely.

The head four wives had played an important part in the daily organization and feeding of the colony. Their skills and leadership became better as the days progressed. Renedo was still the leader. She appointed the late Joncar's wife, Bonestra, in charge of meat and its preparation. Renedo helped her to gather and prepare all the other foods. Philcor's wife, Estra, was put in charge of regulating the duties of the older men and young women. Jealon's wife, Movenea, was the supervisor of clean up and packing the foods and utensils for each trip. The women quickly went about the business of organizing the camp and cave. The older men prepared a suitable fire pit and built a fire. The rest of the women began preparing for the evening meal.

Kuballar gathered all the leaders to the edge of the wide expanse. He gathered them at the jagged edge, overlooking the trail they would use in the following days. He pointed down to the canyon below, saying, "Pillas and I have conferred on the next journey ahead of us. He has assured me that there will be no danger in our many days of travel through the Bacaris Canyon. Comptes remembers that the navigation through there was smooth and pleasant. I remember many fresh water holes with nuts and berries all around. There was also plenty of small game to hunt that tasted really excellent roasted over the fire. It will be a good contrast from what we have just been through."

The many family leaders talked and, some, even murmured amongst themselves. Again, Oxenya and Ouspa, were among the biggest contributors to antagonism. After many explanations and some family leaders, who suddenly got tired of their wrangling, started shouting, Oh Way Gupah! Oh Way Gupah!" Soon, there was silence. Ohpeya, hearing all the rhetoric, spoke up, I have been talking to many family

AGE OF ICE

leaders. They all are in compliance with what Kuballar has said. We all agree that the future looks good, so let us go forward with no more antagonism!" It was as if everyone was waiting for someone to shut the big mouths up. All began to shout, "Upah Wishuga, Upah Wishuga, over and over. It soon was apparent to the dissenters, that they were in the minority, so they quietly slithered away into the background.

It was late in the afternoon when the leaders returned. The meal was ready and all gathered around the open area, in front of the cave. As they ate, the family leaders relayed the message of hope to their families. There were smiles and laughter all around as the colony, suddenly became lighthearted and cheerful. That evening around the fire, many broke out in dancing, shouting and chanting, both for their lost loved ones and the good news that was filled with promise for the trail ahead.

It was late and dark before they all settled down to rest for the night. No one seemed to worry about attacking beasts for Comptes had assured them that they didn't come up this high and they had a second parameter guard just to be sure. It was a crisp night and colder than they were experiencing. Some of the people dug out their extra furs from their packs. The moon came out and shone brightly over the rocks.

The guards were happy to be on duty on this beautiful night. Even some of the women did not retreat to the cave, but spent time with their husbands, watching the beauty of the night. Ohnik and his son, Kuballar, were two such people. Ohnik found his wife Renedo and they found a secluded spot far away from the colony to watch the stars. Kuballar found his wife Kistra, also, and found another secluded corner.

There, they were about to do more than watch the stars. Although Ohnik and Kuballar were typical Age

AGE OF ICE

of Icemen, but since their transformation, they had become very different. A typical Age of Ice male would always try to dominate the female. To tame her, he would grab her, drag her into his cave, and have sex with her by force. If another male tried to intervene, he would challenge the intruder and, either kill him or, chase him away in humiliation and disgrace. He then felt a sense of greatness and honor. He normally would climb a high ledge, pound his chest and shout victory cries to the sky. The female also felt honored to be accepted by such a strong, fierce, and loyal man. This was always the way it was in Feriandimal until the Glowing Ball of Knowledge transformed them forever.

It was this factor, the trauma of the past days, and this beautiful night, that led Ohnik and his wife to find a secluded spot, far from the fire and the others in the colony. Ohnik led her tenderly by the arm away from the guards, making sure that no one saw them. He found a nice flat area that was behind the open area. Once there, he gently put his arm around Renedo and tenderly told her how he felt and how much he cared for her. She was so astonished by his action, that she broke tradition, as well, and told him, also, how much he meant to her. Soon, they were feeling emotions most Age of Icemen never feel. a sensuous desire for each other surged through their bodies and these became so emotionally overwhelming that they tore each others clothes off and made mad, passionate love.

When they were through and rested, they hugged and kissed each other tenderly. Renedo looked lovingly in Ohnik's eyes and said, "Ohnik, this is something we both must treasure. No couple has found this love between them before. Our love making was not for children or lust to prove superiority, it was loving and tender. We will never be the same Age of Icemen again." Ohnik looked back into her eyes, tenderly and replied, "Yes, you are so right. The feelings that roared through us has never happened before and they were so strong, that I know we will

AGE OF ICE

be changed forever, and I might add, for the good." He hugged and kissed her tenderly again.

Unknown to Ohnik and Renedo, Kuballar and Kistra had been feeling the same closeness and they too found a secluded spot away from the colony. They too intended to just look at the stars together but when the two hugged and kissed, when Kuballar tenderly told Kistra how much she meant to him, the same surge of passion went through them, as went through Ohnik and Renedo. Soon the passion of hugging and kissing turned to more emotional activities. They too began to tear each others cloths off. They stood naked before each other. The bright glimmering moonlight, trickled across her full and sumptuous breasts. Kuballar had never stopped to notice how beautiful her body was. he stared at her for a moment and then his desire for her got the best of him and him reached out and fondled her breast, ever so tenderly. Kistra had never had these feelings inside her either and she pressed their naked bodies close as she kissed him. Soon they too were on the ground, making mad and passionate love. This new and exciting era of romance would eventually spread throughout the colony and start the process of building a grand and glorious social order, one that even Theasium would smile over.

The next day all of the colony seemed closer to each other and more joyful. The worst seemed behind them and the Promised Land loomed closer and closer. They all went about their duties lighthearted and in good spirits. Even Oxenya and Ouspa seemed content, at least for the moment. Many discussed their past experiences and what the journey ahead would have in store for them. The leaders were busy too, going over the next few days plans. They wanted to be sure each responsible person knew what to do. The day was real enjoyable for all and they got in their needed rest. The morning was routine. The leaders gathered all the families in proper sequences. They packed their supplies on the

AGE OF ICE

supply carriers and checked to make sure all was aboard. Comptes was now rested and recovered from the injuries of the avalanche, so he was again the leader of the colony. He led them down the trail past the high jagged cliffs. Soon the rough and rocky trail became smoother and less steep. Ahead was the most uneventful experience of the entire trip. The trail remained smooth and the incline, gradual. There were no jagged rocks, no turbulent landslides, no ferocious animals attacking, only slow curving trails that descended, ever so gradual, down to the canyon floor.

As they descended the landscape returned its beauty. Bushes full of flowers dotted the landscape, as did huge tall trees with large overhanging canopies. There were nuts and fruit everywhere. The people all stopped many times to look and enjoy and to pick and eat till full. Soon, before midday, they were at the canyon floor.

It was close enough for the midday meal so the women took out the supplies and prepared the meal. Comptes went over the route with the other Adventurers. Comptes spoke, "You remember that we had trouble finding an exit out of the canyon. We had to double back three times because we hit dead ends. "Your right," replied Kuballar, "but you are the expert navigator. What do you think is the correct route?" Comptes thought for a moment and replied, "Well, if my memory serves me well, I remember that there were three separate canyons in one. The first two led to no where. Each of those canyons had higher and higher cliffs to climb until at last there was nothing but high walls. The third had a river bed that wound through the canyon to the valley below and into Megar Flats. "Yes," said Pillas, "I remember now too. There were a lot of high rocks covering the entrance so it was hard for us to find, but once we limbed over those rocks, the river and canyon trail became visible to us." It was as though a light went off in Kuballar's head as he interrupted, "Oh yes, and the water was

AGE OF ICE

clear and ice cold. We caught many fish with our bare hands on the way through." They all agreed that this was the trail and they told Comptes to follow his instincts.

When everyone was packed and ready, Comptes led them though the first section of canyon. There was only one canyon with high walls and it was easy to follow. Soon they came to a large expanse where the three canyons branched off. Comptes stopped and examined the surroundings. The other Adventurers conferred with him. The two dead end canyons were easy to see their openings, but the right one had a rock washed up high in its opening and the water ran underground at this point. They in one direction, then another, still they could not find it. Pillas who was quiet through most of the decisions, spoke, "My senses are getting bad vibrations in that direction!" He pointed to where the rocks were piled high. "They are telling me danger lies that way, so the armaflorvia must be in that direction and so, the trail must be there too." They climbed the pile of rocks and sure enough, there was the river, flowing out of the canyon wall and down a winding river bed. "Hurrah!" shouted the Adventurers. "There it is!" They climbed down and gave the good news to the others.

It was getting late and the sun would soon set, even though there was no cave nearby, they decided to camp here in this open expanse. The team members by now had many different experiences in a variety of situations, so they were very adept at setting up camp here. There would be extra guards here, in the open, and they would place the second brigade of axe hunters on the outer edge. As they prepared the evening meal others spent time conversing and planning future events. So too, The Adventurers took this time to bone up on the more serious events that were about to unfold. Kibling was first to speak, "You know, the next coming days will be very dangerous, especially for the children. I still have scars on my back and arms as prove of this danger." "You're right," answered Pillas, "even now, I sense their presence. They know we are here for I saw two large black spots, high in the sky, circling and watching our every move. Then they left and I guess they went back to report." Kuballar was quick to respond, "Why didn't you tell us of this before?" Pillas was also quick in his response, "Because, I wasn't sure at first just what they were and I didn't want to upset the colony so soon after the last tragedy. Now, my senses are strong and I fear they are waiting for us to come to them." Comptes entered the discussion with, "You are wise, there Pillas. Remember that some of the families panicked before, because of danger. It will be wise of us to plan a route that will protect the colony as much as we can."

They sat there for a long time just dwelling on the many possibilities and which would be the best solution. Suddenly, Kuballar said, Comptes, you remember those large grostiks, with the big canopies?" "Well yes, now that you mention it, I do." "Well, when we were attacked, we found refuge behind those tall grostiks and from behind them, we could counter attack and drive them away." Comptes responded with, "You are right, in fact, I marked out stones where we did this and I am sure I can find them." Kibling was shocked at his remarks and said, "I thought Arteson and I were the only ones who was marking and painting things, but I must admit, that was very clever of you."

Kuballar got up and looked out at the people preparing the campsite. The others continued in their discussion. He walked over to the edge, where the river was flowing. He studied how interestingly the water gurgled out of the cliff, spurting its contents out in white bubbly foam, then churning its way down the river bed, splashing and gurgling as it hit each of the rocks in the bed. "How strange," he thought, "this new environment. I know that I still have much to learn." Then his eyes gazed, upwards, toward the sky. He thought, for a moment,

AGE OF ICE

that he could see some small black specks, flying in the distance, but the more he stared, the more he thought it was his imagination. A strong fear went through him and he quickly returned to the others and said, "What if the armaflorvia find their way here or if we elude them by hiding in the tall trees, and they are clever enough to go in the forest and attack us?" Kuballar shot so many questions at them and so fast that they were stunned and couldn't answer him at first. Then, Comptes spoke, "Good point! Then we are sitting ducks, waiting to be picked off, one by one." Pillas said, "Well, maybe that is why I have such vibrations dancing inside me." They all looked off into space for sometime, trying to come up with some solution. Then the Glowing Ball of Knowledge clicked off in Kuballar's mind and he shouted, "That's it!" What's it? Comptes asked him. "The rows of sitting ducks! You see we line the women and children, in layers, deep in the forest. We place layers of hunters with spears and axe men in between them. then, when the armaflorvia attack, the first brigade of spear men will thrust their spear into the flock and slow them down. Then, the axe men will go to work and slice them to ribbons." Pillas spoke up enthusiastically, "You know Kuballar, that might just work. My dad has already trained most of the hunters and guards in the finer points of using the axe. He has more than enough men ready to ward off these flying beasts. My warning sensors have already subsided. I now fear no real danger will come upon us." Kuballar looked at all the others and they looked like they agreed, so he said, "Okay then, its settled. Let us go back to camp. It looks like the evening meal is ready. In the morning we will find the other leaders and report our good news and give them instructions."

There was dancing and music around the ritual fire. After a while of watching and enjoying them, Ohnik got up before the fire and all became quiet to hear what he was about to say. "My good friends, we have

AGE OF ICE

shared some really good times and some really bad
ones. It is customary for the Age of Icemen to pass
on our heritage in story telling. so, I will start
and I want each of you who has a story to tell, to
come before the ritual fire and share it with us."
Many told their stories. It went on into the night,
as each story got more exciting and greater than
the next. Finally, Ohnik stood up and said, "These
stories get better each time I here them but it is
getting late and we must travel tomorrow. Let us
postpone our stories for another night." The colony
really didn't want this to end, particularly the
children, for they looked and listened with wonder,
as each story got more exciting and greater than
the next. But, they all went willingly to bed, some
to sleep sound, but for others, to dream and imagine even greater adventures.

CHAPTER TWELVE:
ATTACK FROM THE SKY & INJURIES ARE HEALED

Kuballar got all the leaders together for an instructional meeting, while the morning meal was being prepared. Kuballar explained what they all discussed and then turned the meeting over to Pillas, saying, "Pillas has been trained as a skillful axe hunter by his dad. He knows more than I do about the fine details of our plan to apprehend the armaflorvia, so, he will lead the instruction." Pillas explained the procedures of the axe tearing to the leaders. Then the four Adventurers divided the group and instructed them on their individual responsibilities. Kuballar was sure, that Both Oxenya and Ouspa, got leadership roles in the various brigades, so they would feel important. After they all were fully instructed, they hurried back to the meal. No one wanted to miss this meal, for they were not sure when they would get a complete meal the next two days.

As they packed, the younger children were given the task to search and pick up everything that the packers did not pack. They did not want to leave anything important behind and also leave a trace of their presence. It was difficult for the older people and the very young to scale the large pile of boulders that stood between them and the river bed. Many of the stronger men assisted them over and onto the flat ground below. Comptes led them down the river bed, that snaked its way through the canyon. There was room enough on each side of the river bank for the colony to walk. Even so, some of the children and younger youth, could not resist the temptation of splashing through the edges of the river. Some even stopped to skip rocks through the water and their parents had to run back and drag them on.

The morning went well and they stopped along various open spots along the way. Philcor was in the

AGE OF ICE

middle of the colony with Ohnik and as they walked, he started a conversation with him. Philcor began, "You know Ohnik, I must confess to you, that at first, I too had doubts about the success to this expedition, but these sons of ours really have come through for us. They seem to know every detail of the trail to the Promised Land. They have found solutions to all our problems. Even though we have some loss of life it's been better than many of our hunting expeditions ever were. I only hope these next two days are equally as successful." They kept walking awhile and Ohnik replied, "I am glad that you are on board with us. Yes, these sons of ours are really special. They have found a plan for every dilemma. I only hope the hunters will respond as well when those flying beasts attack us." "My men are well trained and ready," replied Philcor, "they will know what to do and if the spear men are as good, we shall have plenty of flying carcasses and meat to feast on for the final trip." They both continued down the trail deep in thought. Finally Ohnik responded, "I do not know if I have ever told you this but since we all have encountered the Glowing Ball of Knowledge, we all are different. I can see good in people. I choose wiser moves and I even show a sense of love and affection for my family. I see you too, Philcor, becoming a better and wiser person. Your invention of the axe and skill using it, would not have happened otherwise. I am sure we would not be here walking down this river bed if we had not encountered that ball." "Yes, Ohnik, I must confess that I would not have done all this by myself," Philcor replied, "I am sure that there is something higher, greater, and bigger out there guiding us."

The colony descended to the lower level of the canyon trail. There were trees and thick bushes to the right of them. Straight ahead they could see the opening to Megar Flats. They could see the brightness of the sunshine through the opening. As they got closer, they could see the sun reflecting, brightly, in the fields of green, red, and purple

AGE OF ICE

grasses. There were fields of flowers in all directions. Comptes stopped and let everyone regroup. Some wanted to run out into the fields but the leaders cautioned them, reminding them of the danger of the armaflorvia. A few parents had to chase after their children, who were even more tempted to romp in the tall green grasses.

After all had rested and were refreshed, Kuballar got up on a large ledge and spoke to the colony, "My fellow Age of Ice families. We have made great progress on our journey so far. Sure, we have had some casualties, we have lost some loved ones and we are sorry for that. The expedition has been very successful, thanks to the expert work of tour leaders and hunters. You also, as a colony, have performed well. We are almost to the Promised Land of beauty, the one that we have told you about. There is just one more perilous place before we arrive at our new home. It is just ahead of us. There are flying beasts in the sky that have very sharp teeth and claws. They fly high up over the Megar Flats. Going through there would be easier and faster but those demons would see us and attack us. Many of us would be injured or killed. To prevent this we have discussed this with all the leaders of the colony. They will instruct each of you and guide you through the mura grostiks. It will be hard for many of you. The mura grostik is very dense and thick with thorns that can scratch and cut you. If we are careful and take our time, we shall get through with little discomfort. It is just two days of travel to Much Ohts Canyon. There we will regroup and find the final trail to The Promised Land. We found no perils there in our first adventure. So, I speak to you now, that you may be strong and follow what your family leaders tell you."

When Kuballar had finished speaking, the leaders organized the colony for the trek through the forest. They followed Comptes and Kuballar into the thicket. It was really slow going at first for no one had experienced a forest this thick and thorny.

AGE OF ICE

In places they axe men had to chop their way through. There were unexpected lizard-like creatures and large snakes that slithered through the trees. The lizard-like creatures puffed themselves up, screeched and showed their teeth. The snakes hissed their warning as they slithered through the trees. At first the leaders thought that they would prove a greater risk, but soon, they found them to be harmless.

They had completed more than a half day and still they had only gone about one fourth the way through. Because of the difficulty, it seemed to them, that they should be already through. They were really disappointed to learn how little progress they made. They found a clearing, just inside the forest and stopped for a much deserved rest. They posted the guards and the rings of spear and axe men in the outer circles to be on the safe side.

As they were resting and nourishing the colony, the armaflorvia came streaking in unannounced. These birds had eyes like our hawks and could see the tiniest prey from high in the sky. There was a slight opening in the dense forest for the birds to see them resting. They streaked down from high in the sky and hit before anyone was aware of their presence. Luckily, they gathered the women and children in the deeper part of the clearing. The guards blew the warning horns and the hunters prepared their spears for the kill. One by one, the armaflorvia flew in for the attack and the hunters were ready. Jealon, Ohnik, and Kibling's spear men formed three brigades. Jealon had the outer most brigade. If they missed some, then Ohnik's brigade would attack, and if they still missed some, Kibling's brigade would be there, to wound them enough, so that Philcor's axe men could chop them to pieces.

The first armaflorvia came in fast and low. The first brigade threw their spears and only two were hit, while many bounced off the armor of the birds.

AGE OF ICE

The second brigade armed and carefully aimed at the softer, inner part of the bird's neck or upper chest cavity. They threw their spears and many more hit their mark. Some of the spears entered the inner crevices of the neck and deep into the inner part of the bird's throat. An agonizing and loud screech came out of their mouths as they fell to the ground in agony and pain. These beasts fell short of their target, thrashing around, rolling and twisting in torment, trying to remove the spears. Immediately, the axe men rushed up and subdued the birds. Some grabbed their wings, while others, grabbed its beak and tied it to a nearby tree. The others, started hacking at their necks, finding and separating the skull bones. They were careful so that they could save the meat for the final journey. Soon many of the birds lay still, their heads in the axe men's hands. The women and children cheered, as they pulled the carcasses to the side and waited for another attack.

They stood silent for awhile, hoping that the others had seen what they did and would retreat. But that was not the case. Within a short duration of time, the second flock of armaflorvia circled the colony, saw what happened to their first comrades, and then, to see exactly where their real targets were. They came in higher and as it came to the first brigade, they swerved, dodged, and darted, avoiding most of the spears. The second brigade stood ready and flung their spears. The birds seemed smarter and were watching the first attack, for they too, swerved, dodged, and darted but were higher and some got by the first brigade's attack. The second brigade was ready and they thrust their spears at the on coming armaflorvia. All hit their mark and they fluttered to the ground to be met by the axe men. The two of the armaflorvia saw their targets and went in with strong pursuit. As they flew in for the victory, Ohnik, jumped up and thrust his spear into one of the bird's throat. Green liquids began spurting out of the wound, but the momentum of the birds speed and its rampant

AGE OF ICE

determination, the bird flew right through the axe men brigade and into the group of women and children. One women saw it coming and put herself as a shield, in front of the children. The beastly bird had enough strength left to thrust it's outer wing claws directly at the women. His momentum, tore holes into her, thrusting her to the ground in agony and pain. Philcor and some of his men quickly dashed over and subdued the bird. As they held it down, two axe men chopped its head off. The bird, though dead, instinctively, twisted, and rolled repeatedly on the ground until all life left it and it lay still. The second bird was luckier and found an unsuspecting child. It quickly thrust it talons into it and was off into the air. Before it could get high enough to escape, Philcor smashed his axe through the birds head, sending the bird and the child rolling aimlessly unto the ground. The men rushed up and finished off the bird, while others, picked up the child and rushed it to Soothsay. They quickly pulled the carcass aside and waited for the third attack. The other armaflorvias, watching what was happening, decided this wasn't worth all the losses and flew back, out through the canopy, and back to their nests. The people concerned, immediately ran to the assistance of the wounded women and the child. The rest checked others around her and found no other casualties. Her husband, who was one of the axe men, came up and saw his wife in pain. Immediately he cried out in anguish for help. Soothsay, after treating the child who had miner wounds, went to the women's aid. He had a lot of experience back in Feriandimal. Although there weren't many plants in the frozen and rocky terrain of Feriandimal, he was able to find a few plants on the warm side of rock crevices. Some of them he found, even helped stop the flow of blood. Here there was an abundant amount of herbs. He had gathered many on the way, just to be prepared. He did not have the exact herb on him, so he quickly searched the forest for a substitute. He had a number of his helpers to help him. He gave instructions, and soon, they found what they were looking

DANGER FROM THE SKY

ARMAFLORVIA

AGE OF ICE

for. He bit into the leaves and tasted them. "Sure enough, you have found the right herb," remarked Soothsay to his helpers. "This is exactly like the ones at the ice fields, only sweeter." He and his helpers quickly went over to where the wounded woman was lying, still in agony and pain. They picked her up gently and laid her on one of his fur skins. He tended to her arm first. It was bleeding profusely and she was loosing a lot of blood. He asked one of his assistants to help him. First, he chewed the leaves into a liquid pulp. Then he told the assistant to hold her arm upright and tight. He sprinkled the liquid pulp into her deep wounds. He showed his assistant how to hold the wound shut. As the assistant held it tightly together, Soothsay wrapped some of the whole leaf tightly around the wound on her arm. Then he took skin ropes from his belt and tied the bundled wound together. Soon, the bleeding on her arm stopped, and the woman's crying anguish slowed to mere sobs. He then attended her other, less severe puncture wounds, that the bird's claws had made. He gave some leaves to his assistants and some he kept and he showed them how to soften the leaves in their mouth for application to the wounds. Once they were soft enough, Soothsay took the leaves and rolled them into proper sizes and placed them into each puncture wound, tying it up so it would heal. He watched over her for some time. Soon there was a slight smile on her face as her pain was almost gone. All of the people standing by, watching, and some of the leaders, marveled at the skill of Soothsay and the quick recovery of the woman. When soothsay was sure she was alright, he and his assistants checked all the children and any others that might have gotten hurt. They found some frightened but no one else was injured.

The leaders also checked the entire colony to make sure they were all okay. Kuballar sent out scouting parties, in all directions, to make sure that the armaflorvia had really left. Kibling went a step further and took his trusted men to the far

AGE OF ICE

corners of Megar Flats. "I will make sure that those evil beasts are not lying in wait for us as we journey forward. We will return on the nusea hence. You camp here till we return." They took weapons of axe, spear and knife, food and blankets and left. "That is a brave gesture, Kibling, my fiend," responded Kuballar. Yes, we will camp here and wait, news of your return." As they departed, Comptes replied, "May those that are watching over us, guard and keep you safe." They waved and disappeared into the dense mura grostiks of Megar Flats, traveling in the route that Comptes had laid out for them. It took them two full nusea hands to reach the clearing of the woods. Once there, they were extra cautious in their travel in the open territory of the flats, traveling along the edge of the woods. They watched intently, to make sure that none of the armaflorvia was waiting in hiding for them. By nusea down, they had already scouted half of the flats. On the far side, they spotted about ten armaflorvia, that were high up and flying towards the other mountain range. They discussed this and decided that the birds had sensed too much danger and left for a better location. It was almost dark and they found a suitable campsite and lodged there for the night.

The camp was all established and Kuballar took the other leaders, to the edge of camp, for another planning session. He addressed them with, "Men, this encounter with the birds went better than any of us thought. If Kibling and his men bring back good news, the remaining trip should be pleasant and successful." Ohnik asked his son, "Tell us, son, just how far do we have to go yet?" Kuballar looked at his father, strangely, but replied, "Once we leave here, it will take us many more light orders. Much Ohts Canyon is very long and tedious in some places. When we reach the end, we must camp for a number of light orders. The trails are hidden and hard to find, so we must send a search party to find the correct passage over the last set of mountains." Oxenya listened as usual with a questioning mind. He went off to one side and began whispering to Ouspa and a number of other leaders. Ohpeha and Questoma were part of the leaders in the group and when Ohpeha had heard enough he spoke up loudly to Kuballar, "It seems that there are some that still have questions and doubts. I ask your leave that all of us may further discuss these events that you say are still to come." Kuballar looked at him a little angry at first but then replied, " I had thought that all the doubts were behind us. Now, do you plan further doubts and disruption?" Ohpeha got a real sad expression on his face and looked down to the ground, saying nothing in return. Questoma quickly spoke up for the group, "We beg your pardon, oh Great Kuballar, but we intend no such disruption or descent, rather, only to further answer the questions of some doubters so we all may work together in harmony. Kuballar returned to his normal pleasant self, after hearing Questoma and replied, "Please forgive for what I have just said. Yes, if you wish, I beg you go and find this harmony. The leaders broke up in groups and discussed what Kuballar had just reported. While they were in discussion, Ohnik came up to his son and said, "I know you looked at me strangely for asking that question, but I heard Oxenya and his son, Ouspa trying to stir up more unrest. For awhile I had thought to keep our plans secret until we carry them out but seeing their reactions, I now think that the more all the leaders know, the more they will trust you and the rest of us." Kuballar stood thinking for a moment and then said to his father, "Good point, Father, I only hope you are right and we finally get all the leaders on our side." Comptes was listening to them and couldn't help but comment, "I beg your forgiveness for listening in on your conversation but I must reply to what you just said." Kuballar quickly turned to him with, "Why of course Comptes, anything you have to say I will sure consider as worthy." Comptes smiled at his remarks and replied, "It is just that I know Questoma, well as does your father, and I know he will surely make the leaders come to harmony."

CLOSE UP MAP OF JOURNEY'S FINAL TRAIL

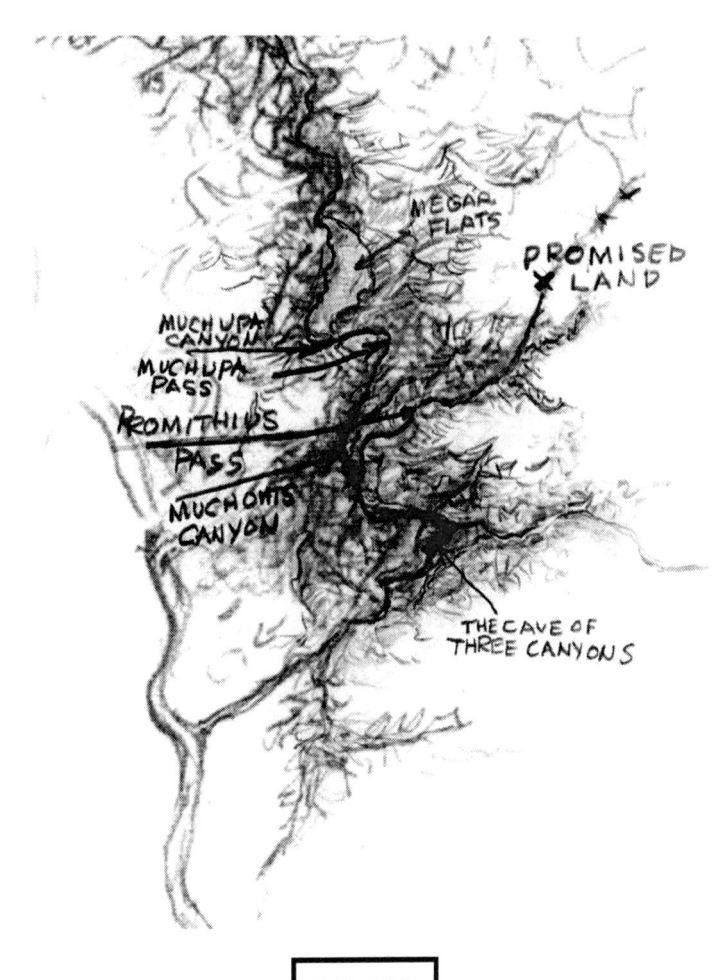

CHAPTER THIRTEEN:
A NEW BEGINNING AS THE JOURNEY ENDS

The family leaders finished their discussion and Ohpeya spoke for them, "We have discussed what Kuballar has just said and decided that up to this point, the Adventurers and the other head leaders, have got us through dangerous territory and other perils with only minor casualties. With such a short distance and our growing faith in the leaders, we accept and stand behind Kuballar and the Adventurers." They returned to the camp and found that the evening meal was ready. As they walked back, Kuballar remarked to his dad and Comptes, saying, "You were right in your understanding of Questoma and the family leaders. It sure is nice to have a vote of confidence for a change." Ohnik smiled and put his arm around his son as they walked.

It was late morning when Kibling and his men arrived back in camp. The guards saw them coming and blew their horns. Some hunters thought that the birds had returned and grabbed their weapons and ran forward for the attack. When they saw Kibling, with a smile on his face, they lowered their weapons and ran back to camp shouting, "They are back! Upah Wishuga! Upah Wishuga!" They all gathered around Kibling and waited for him to speak.

Kibling found a large, flat stump near by. He climbed up on it and began to speak, "My good friends. I have very good news for you. We searched the entire Megar Flats and only saw one sign of the armaflorvia and they were headed away from us, to another mountain range. After hearing this joyous news, the entire colony broke out into celebration.

Kibling saw all the excitement that was going on and thought this was the best time to introduce his new musical instrument. During the trip, he had found a new large vine, on one of the trails. He

AGE OF ICE

cut, dried, and stored it away in his pack. Evenings, when he wasn't busy, he whittled away at it, turning it into, what he hoped would be a new musical instrument. He hollowed out the center and put various sizes of holes along its top. He would experiment with the hole sizes by blowing and carving until it sounded right to him. Now he got it out of his pack and was ready to make his debut with it.

He entered the circle of colony members that were watching the dancers and those blowing horns and playing drums. He stepped into their area and started playing. It sounded like a beautiful flute. Soon everyone stopped and listened to him. When he was through they all cheered and yelled, "More! More!" He played until his mouth got sore and then the dancing continued. The celebration and dancing went on late into the afternoon.

The Adventurers met with the leaders and discussed the next days journey. Kuballar spoke to them saying, "Men we have still, a day and a half journey through this thorny thicket. Then we will leave Megar Flats and climb Much Ups Pass. It is a days travel over the pass and into Much Ohts Canyon." Comptes the navigator was first to reply, "Kuballar, my good friend, you are right about your memory but this thorny and thick mura grostiks might take longer to get through." Pillas immediately broke in, "Yes, it just may take longer and I also sense an evil presence up ahead in the thicker portion. I suggest that we take extra precautions." After listening to both of his Adventurer friends, Kibling spoke, "I have some good news that may shed a light on this travel plan. In our travels, looking for those flying beasts, we discovered two things that will help us. First, the journey is much shorter to the Much Ups Canyon Pass. Second, as I have told you, those armaflorvia have left for a better hunting grounds and now, pose us no threat. I suggest that we journey through the Megar Flats and save valuable time and much energy. I also heard you, Pillas, say that you sensed danger in the last of the deeper and darker mura grostiks. If we avoid them altogether, we will also avoid the danger." Pillas thought for a moment and replied, "Kibling, what good thinking and observations. I did not connect my vibrations of danger with just the darker mura grostiks, but if you are right, then that surely would be a better way for us to go." Then let us return to the colony. We will talk it over with all the leaders and then, make our final decision." They did just that and after a series of discussions, they decided to follow Kibling's route. It was Ohnik who settled their minds when he said to them, "After all we were attacked even here in this terrible thicket. Pillas senses danger up ahead in the deeper thick area. If it is much easier in the flats, than I am all for it."

The next morning Comptes and Kuballar, led them out of the dark, thorny forest and into the grassy Megar Flats. They sent scouts ahead to make sure that it was safe. They found no danger and proceeded into the flats. It was really enjoyable walking here, compared to the forest. The grass was soft and smooth and there was flowers everywhere and the air was filled with their delightful scents. It did not take them even a day to get down to the opening of the canyon that leads to the Much Ups Pass. They saved almost a day's journey and countless quells of energy.

They stopped just inside the wall of the canyon. Comptes and two of his scouts went ahead to find a location to camp. They came back to report the finding of a secure cave, big enough, for the entire colony. It was less than a hand of the nusea away and it was still early. They lazily set up camp and started the evening meal. The meal was extra special for many, because they were serving the armaflorvia for the main course. It was a pleasure to eat these evil monsters, after they caused so much turmoil and suffering to the colony. The woman who was injured by the bird, enjoyed chewing on its

AGE OF ICE

meat, and she even gnawed on the bones. They all felt pleasurably full and retreated to the ritual fire. Here, they insisted that Kibling play his magic tube again. He agreed and started playing. the notes came out like tranquil messages of love. Everybody around the fire got close and listened as he played his magic to them. Ohnik and his wife found it so romantic that they secretly disappeared for a rendezvous of love. There were many others that night, that would expand the population of the colony. The performance continued and Kibling was mesmerizing those that were still in attendance. Pillas, who made some stone hammers and stretched skins over hollow logs, also got in the act as well. He began to keep beat with Kibling and soon, they were in harmony with each other. The men and women began to join in and danced and chanted. The children then joined in. Everyone was full of joy and harmony late into the night.

During the night clouds filled the sky and it started to rain. There was no danger of flooding, for they were on high ground. The rain was heavy and across the pass, the river began to rise. In the morning it was still cloudy and wet as the women prepared the morning meal. It was difficult, for the older men, packing up the provisions, for they could not put the bundles outside because of the mud. They had problems stacking them in the narrow cave and still leave room for walking. It seemed like even here, heavy, inclement weather affects the emotions of people, for as the hunters left the cave their spears hit the bundles, knocking some down. Both the old men and hunters were angry and exchanged words.

The hunters left to find food for the trip and the head leaders met to coordinate the next journey over the pass and through the next canyon. "Men, this is the last journey through a canyon before we reach the Promised Land. When we set out, we will climb a pass that will be easy to maneuver. It will also have a breath taking view on top. The grade

AGE OF ICE

down is not steep and there are few rocks to hinder our walk. When we reach Much Ohts Canyon, we will find a safe and enclosed environment. Only in heavy rains, will there be some danger of rising water, for a river runs through the full course of the canyon. The river banks are wide and flat in most places, making it an easy route to travel. The only problem we had was finding the pass that leads to the Promised Land. There are three branch canyons at the end. The middle one leads to a high cliff and dead ends. We took this route the first time and lost two days. The river follows the second canyon and it leads to the right and away from our destination. The other canyon's trail is hard to find and we will have to send out scouts to find it. We will camp there till the scouts come back and report. This is my best accounting of the next events and I will let Comptes fill you in on things that I missed." Comptes replied, " Kuballar is too modest. What he just said is exactly as we will find it, and besides, this time it will be easier for we have left trail markers on the trail. Kibling carved interestingly shaped wood markers along the way that I'm sure will be easy to find. After a few questions, they all returned to the main camp.

They came into camp to see all the women in an uproar. Some were screaming and others yelling for help. They discovered to Comptes's surprise, that his pregnant wife, Celestra, had broken her water and had started in labor. Renedo saw what was happening and ran for Soothsay. As soon as she had told him of what was happening, he came running. He checked her condition and then, made all the necessary preparations for birth. His assistants were out on the hunt, so he enlisted some women and older men. He gave them instructions to what they each were to do and they quickly carried them out.

It was tradition of the Age of Icemen, for the father of a new born, to go high up in the mountains and wait. Comptes took his son, Navitona along and they journeyed up the mountain trail to a high

COMPTES AND NAVITONA IN THE MOUNTAIN TOP PRAYER

AGE OF ICE

lookout point. Here, tradition told him to chant and stare at the sky. Together, Comptes and Navitona leaned on some rocks and began their chant. They stared at the sky and soon, as they chanted, over and over the same verse they were taught, they became mesmerized and their eyes started rolling and there were images before them that they could not comprehend.

Trolldar, the wizard, was near by and heard their chants. He immediately sensed what was happening and made himself transparent. He positioned himself before the birth and absorbed all thoughts of the new child's present condition and future events. He then returned to the mountain. He quickly began to appear before Comptes and his son. They thought they were hallucinating, but Trolldar started to appear before them as a glowing light. Then he imaged himself into the glowing light and addressed them saying, "Fear not, Comptes, for unto you is born a healthy son. He will grow in knowledge and stature, even beyond your dreams. He will be leader of men and establish a great place where people will follow him and give him homage. You will name him Baulic. Trolldar, then released his image and the glowing form was gone. He chose not to tell them of the future scenes. One such scene was really bad. It was a dictator named Baulstar. In their linage, he saw him joining Doomagnon and developing many evil acts. These acts all were made to eventually conquer all of Dimensia 4. "I will not journey there," he said to himself, "that is for another time."

Comptes and his son screamed and thrust their heads between their legs. Both asked the questions in their minds, "What was this glow from the sky and who was in it?" They sat there mesmerized for a long time, neither one, wanting to talk first. After awhile, they uncovered their faces and looked up. There was nothing in front of them, except the rocks and other landscape. Comptes turned to his son and asked, "Did you not see that image in the glowing light?" Navitona looked into his father's eyes and said, "Oh yes, Father, I too saw and heard what that glowing image said."

They both sat there by the rocks contemplating all they had just heard and saw. Comptes turned and took Navitona by the hand and said, "This surely is a sign and a command from above. What is up there, I do not know, but I do know this, we both saw this great image and he told me of my son's welfare and gave him a name. This now I am certain of, is that there is greater forces than ourselves out there and they are trying to direct us." Navitona replied, "Yes, Father, you are so right! I even heard the older men, on the trail, telling each other that they believed there was a greater force out there in the sky, directing us." Comptes looked skyward and said back to Navitona, "Then it is settled. We must accept this force who is helping us. We must set up a special place where we can honor them and tell them how we feel. Navitona turned to his father and said, "Yes, this I see as good. I will help you do this when we get to our new land."

Soon, the message came up the trail that Comptes's son was born. They quickly retreated, down, to the place of birth. When Comptes arrived, Soothsay was holding the baby and trying to quiet him from his screaming. Some of the women were attending to Celestra and following Soothsay's directions. It was customary for the father only to observe his new born and not hold it until the child could walk. Comptes broke all traditions and walked up to Soothsay, took his son and held him in his arms. He began to rock and say soothing sounds to him and softly chanted, "Hush my son, don't you cry, for you are Baulic the Great." Soon, the child quieted and fell fast asleep in Comptes's arms. Soothsay, looking on, replied, "Surely this is a sign of great things in your family." Soothsay didn't understand why he just said that, but Trolldar, at this moment, was above, directing thoughts into his mind. This wasn't the first time either, for it was

AGE OF ICE

on accident, that Soothsay had studied and discovered all these healing remedies and procedures and this will not be the only time that Trolldar would find it necessary to intervene.

The leaders now knew that it would be impossible to leave the next day so they decided to set up camp again and stay at least two more days or until Celestra and the baby could travel. In the meantime, the camp had another reason to celebrate and celebrate they did! Even the stoic Jealon broke down and danced around the ritual fire circle. Kibling and Arteson as usual joined the group to help in the celebration. There were many others that had made make-shift instruments and joined in on the celebration.

With extra time on their hands the hunters went out on hunting expeditions to shore up the food supply. It seemed like the arrival of a new born brought them luck for the hunters came back the next afternoon with great success. They dropped their hunting catch in front of the cave and all were amazed. Among the catch were some kupabins, a swordenfin tubres, and many goulas. It was a new animal, that they found in the high country. It looked a little like our wild goats. After all the enthusiasm of the catch subsided, they dragged their catch away from the camp and started their process of cleaning, preparing, and preserving the meat. Some of the hunters and older men, found stones, deep in the cave, that tasted like salt. They were soft and easy to crush. The colony had almost ran out of the original salt they brought along from Feriandimal and this was another stroke of good fortune. They brought it to the hunters, who had cut most of the meat in strips and now they rubbed the salt and some herbs that Soothsay had collected. They wrapped the meat in skins, tied them securely, and set them aside to cure. They now had enough meat for many days travel.

On the third day both Celestra and her baby seemed

THE HUNTERS CATCH THEIR PREY

KUPABIN

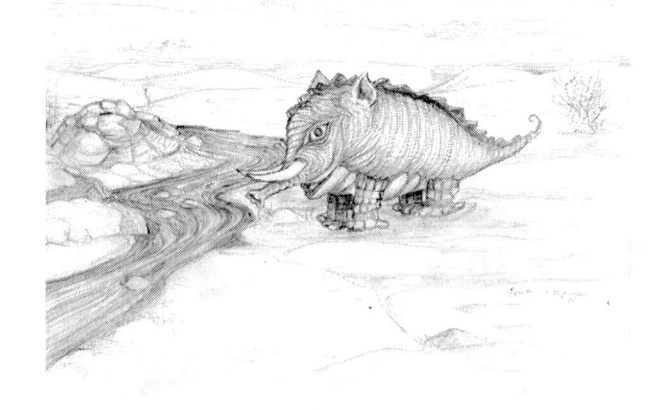

SWORDENFIN TUBRES

GOULA

AGE OF ICE

healthy and fit enough to travel. The older men packed all their supplies, while the families prepared for the journey. All the guards and leaders got into their proper places and Kuballar gave the signal to commence. Comptes led the way and he was beaming as a proud father. Even some of the men, smiled as they saw his joy. They headed up the trail to the summit pass. As they got higher, they stopped from time to time and the Adventurers pointed out the breath-taking scenes and the canyon below. Once they got to the summit, they stopped to rest and eat. While they were resting, the Adventurers showed them the river where their trail would go. In the distance, they could see the high mountain peaks and ridges of the three canyons below. Comptes pointed to the highest mountain peak and said, "Do you see that high peak over there! That is where the middle canyon lies and where we hit a dead end. We must be sure to avoid that area this time and stay right." They continued enjoying the scenes and imbibing refreshments, until the horn blew to signal that the journey was about to commence.

Comptes led them down the back side of the pass toward the river canyon below. After a short rest, Comptes then led them into the river canyon. The river bed, was wide and rocky. There was plenty of water flowing for it had rained heavily in the mountains for two days. The run off filled river with rushing, bubbling water. It was a good source of water, both for drinking and cooking. Although this river seemed a blessing for abundant water, they soon found that it was a nuisance. Soon, when the river narrowed, it made forging it almost impossible for the young and old. But again, the Adventurers found ways of helping the young and elderly cross. After a number of difficult crossings, the river got shallower and even Celestra and her baby had little difficulty. Soon, the river bank widened and all were happy at the ease of travel. It became so inviting that the children again began to stop and play in the water and river banks. The

AGE OF ICE

leaders, sensing this new joy, stopped many times to let them play. It was late afternoon when the colony arrived at the three forks in the canyon. Jealon, Pillas, and Kibling went ahead to find a suitable spot for camping. Jealon had always had a special gift when it came to finding caves. Even way back in his early hunting days, the other hunters always appointed him to find them a cave for the night and he never disappointed them. This special sensing must have been hereditary for Comptes too acquired the special gift of navigation.

The three took the right branch that followed the river for that is where the Adventurers said they found an adequate cave. It didn't take them long to find one for Kibling followed closely along the edge of the river bank and there it was, and he yelled out, "Hey, here it is, one of my markers." He had told them that he had placed it there on their first journey and sure enough, there it was. "When we went the wrong way and had to back track," Kibling continued, "We found a cave. I think it is just a short distance down this river bed to the right." They followed Kibling and as they got closer, Jealon remarked to them, "That series of cliffs up ahead indicate to me caves. The earthen material in those walls always indicate cave formations behind them." Sure enough, as they got closer, there was one of the cave openings. You sure must be right about the earthen material having caves behind them, look to the right farther down, there is another one as well," Kibling told Jealon. Jealon responded to his remarks with, "It is you that should be congratulated for your outstanding memory." Kibling reminded hm that an artist always studies details in his environment closely so he can remember to carve, draw, or paint it later.

Jealon volunteered to stand guard at the entrance while the two young men ventured in to explore its interior. It did not take long before it got so dark that they had to light some torches. They had brought two heavy branches along and wrapped some soft fur skins around one end. They tied it tightly to the branches. Then they soaked them with oil from their pouches and lit them with flint sparks. After adjusting to the lighting conditions, they proceeded further into the cave. Soon they came to a large room with a high ceiling with many smaller side tunnels. These would be suitable for private sleeping quarters for the families. "This is really good," replied Kibling, "My father said that it would be good by its structure and he was right." They looked into a couple of side tunnels and as they were about to enter a third, Pillas whispered, "Stop! I sense some danger up ahead." Kibling quickly asked, "What is it?" Pillas studied the area carefully, concentrating on his inner senses and replied, "I'm not sure exactly what it is but my sensors tell me that the danger is down there in that far tunnel." Kibling got out his knife and held his spear ready for action. Pillas unhooked his axe from his side and held it ready also.

They slowly crept forward and then Pillas quietly pointed to the far corner and whispered, "There it is curled up asleep in the corner that is a borgamuth. Let us stick our torches in these crevices here and sneak up on it. Kibling, when you get near enough stab it with your spear and it will rise up in anger and then I'll whack him with my axe." They crept, ever so slowly forward, not making a sound. As they approached the borgamuth, Kibling raised his spear and thrust it below and just behind the front shoulder. It found its mark and the borgamuth rose upwards with pain and anger in its eyes. It lifted its front claws for an attack. Instead, it lurched high into the air, growled an anguishing cry, and fell to the floor. The spear had penetrated deep into its chest cavity and hit its heart. It was still twisting and groaning in anger and pain as the two went forward to finish it off. But before they could, the borgamuth stopped its groaning and quivering and fell silently in a dead heap. Kibling poked it with his spear as Pillas

AGE OF ICE

held his axe high just in case, but it didn't move. Pillas looked at it and said to Kibling, "You just spoiled all my fun!" They broke out laughing and embraced in their success. Kibling replied to Pillas, We had better leave it here till we bring back the colony." Pillas replied, "Yes, that is a good idea. It will save us time and when we get back I will help you clean, preserve, and store the meat, while the older men can take care of the hide."

They returned to the entrance and told Jealon of their kill and their decision to leave it till they returned with the colony. Jealon responded quickly with, "That won't do for any wild beast will smell the fresh blood and steal it on us! I will stay and guard the borgamuth. You go and fetch the colony!" They all agreed and the two left Jealon while they ventured up the river bed to fetch the colony. "We have found a cave for the colony," replied Pillas, "come! Pick up you gear and follow me!"

When they returned to the cave, Jealon had already started the process of cleaning and dressing the borgamuth. As they were waiting for the colony cave, two of the other hunters had speared some game as well. Comptes helped his father and the two hunters dress the game as Pillas showed the rest of the colony to the interior of the cave. After they had explored enough of the cave, the various families picked out their territory and the colony set up their camp for the night. They posted two guards at the entrance to make sure any other predator such as a borgamuth, demon beast, or sword fin tubres would sneak into the cave at night. Pillas and some other hunters joined Jealon and Comptes and they finished preparing, curing, and packing the meat away. A couple of the hunters dragged the carcass off into the woods and well enough away from camp so that the scavengers could have at it. All were so tired that all went to bed early. There was no celebration that night.

BORGAMUTH

CHAPTER FOURTEEN:
NATURE'S FORCES & THE FRAGILE MAN

During the night the guards noticed that the moon had gone behind the clouds. It wasn't long and it began to rain. By morning it was raining so hard that they couldn't even see across the river. The leaders decided it was impossible to travel and so they stayed in the cave during the down pour. There were little or no holes in the ceiling cave to let smoke out, so they had to limit burning their torches to when it was only a necessity. Those deeper in the cave had to sit in the dark.

They sat there in this condition the entire day and throughout the entire night, as it continued to pour. It finally stopped raining on the second day but the water from the mountain ravines made the river rise rapidly and turned it into a torrent of gushing rapids. The Adventurers and their fathers journeyed up the river bed a ways to check out the conditions. They didn't get very far and the rising river had filled the river banks, at some of the narrower places, above the banks and rising up the cliff walls. The river was so forceful that it was impossible to forge. They were forced to retreat as they watched the river rise before their eyes. They went back to wait it out, for they had no other choice but to stay in the cave and hope the river would not rise too high.

On the third day the sun finally came out. It was bright and clear with not one cloud in the sky. Even though the sky looked promising the river didn't. It was still rising, and now, just a hand width or two from the cave entrance. The guards came running in panic to report this sudden dilemma. The leaders quickly counseled and decided forging the river with its swift current, would be too dangerous. What were they to do. One leader suggested climbing up the cliffs but Kuballar pointed out that those cliffs were too steep for

AGE OF ICE

most of the young and older people in the colony. The only recourse now, was to build up the sand wall high in front entrance higher. They kept piling the sand higher but the river was gaining on them. Then there worst fears happened. The water rose up so high that it started to pour over the high sand wall. Immediately, it started flooding the floor of the cave. The water began to flow throughout the entire cave and started to rise. It started eroding the sand wall and gushed in even stronger. The water was now up to their knees in some areas of the cave. Some of the women and children started panicking. Before the leaders could restore order and stop them, some of the panicking women rushed past them, with their children following behind. They ran in panic, screaming and dashing out of the cave and into the river. As soon as they hit the river, the swift current swept then down stream along with whole trees, broken branches and all other sorts of debris. Others tried to dash out of the cave but now the leaders were able to block their exit. They all stood in the entrance and watched in horror as their loved ones tumbled helplessly down the river and soon they were out of sight and they thought that they would never be seen again. They stood there helpless and all they could see was rushing torrents of water with tons of debris flowing down with the swift and fatal current.

But what really would be their final fate? Unknown to them, Trolldar, sensing this danger, placed himself further down the stream. He saw them dash in and being swept away in the middle of all the debris. As they tumbled towards him, Trolldar quickly thrust his might and force against a tree, causing one of its larger branches to crash down into the stream. It fell directly in front of the terror stricken women and children. Just as they were about to give up to the tumbling waters that kept pulling them under and filling their lungs with dirty, muddy waters, there in front of them were the branches of life. The branches looked like the

TROLLDAR'S RESCUE AT THE THREE CANYON FLOOD

AGE OF ICE

beacons of the night. Quickly, the women grabbed their children and clung tightly to the branches. One by one they helped each other up to the safety of the higher ground. Trolldar again made himself transparent as he looked on with pleasure for he knew that both Theasium and the Highest Being of the Universe would be extra pleased at his quick thinking, fast action, and his successful outcome.

The water did not start to recede until later the next day. The rest of the colony had to stand waist deep in the cave. They were cold, wet, but safe. Many were grieving for their lost ones, for surely, they thought, all had perished. Some of the older and weaker members of the colony felt so tired that they started to slip gradually down into the water. Cries for help was heard and the stronger men came splashing through the caves and tunnel to their aid. Even they felt exhausted and weak as the night progressed.

The next morning the guards were again greeted by a warm and bright sun. As it rose and lit the river, they could see that everything was back to normal. Their eyes couldn't believe it. There before them, just a day ago, were brutal rushing torrents of water, crashing and crushing everything in its path. Now here, in this brightest of mornings, it had receded to its normal level and was a mere trickle. It slowly flowed down the stream as it lazily bubbled and gurgled over the rocks.

The guards couldn't contain themselves. They all ran, splashing through the cave yelling, hollering, and shouting, "The rivers down, we're saved! Upah Wishuga! Upah Wishuga! They yelled. All the leaders ran splashing out to the entrance. They peaked over the high sand wall and sure enough, there was the river back to its normal banks and flowing gently down stream. They too started to jump and dance for joy and shouted, "Upah Wishuga! Upah Wishuga!" Comptes and Navitona quietly thanked the Giver of Life and their helper for this blessed miracle.

AGE OF ICE

Quick," yelled Ohnik, "let us break this sand wall loose so all the water will leave our cave and flow back to the river. They found some axes and stone shovels and started digging. Others dug with their bare hands. Soon the sand wall started to give way and Pillas sensing what could happen, yelled, Not so fast or we all will go rushing out and down the stream with the water. They quickly stopped and let a little at a time flow from the top. Gradually, they dug more away and it increased the flow. By late morning they had all the water, except for some low lying puddles, out of the cave. The women and children cheered and hollered for joy, for now, everything was back to normal. Then they thought of all the lost loved ones who were washed down the turbulent and rushing river and the mood changed to a real low sullen, sadness.

The leaders decided they couldn't do anything for them and if it rained, they might be trapped again, so they dried their belongings and started packing for their journey away from this treacherous river.

There was enough time in the day to get away from the river and find another, more safer, camp. Comptes gathered all the leaders together, gave them quick instructions and started back up the river bed. As they were leaving Pillas was in the rear and suddenly sensed something wrong. He stopped and thought he heard distant yelling sounds of women and children. "Could these be the spirits of our departed," he thought. Then he turned toward the lower part of the river, below the cave and listened more intently. Again, he heard shouting sounds, but this time, more distinct and clear. "By the Greatness of the Being Above," he shouted, "it is our lost loved ones! They are alive!" He turned and blew his warning horn as loud as he could. The entire colony stopped dead in their tracks and turned to see what was the sudden problem that Pillas should warn them. He yelled as loud as he could, "They're alive, our loved ones are down the river waiting for us!" Kuballar, Kibling, and

AGE OF ICE

Philcor quickly caught up to Pillas and they ran down stream to where the group of survivors were yelling and waving at them. To their surprise, all the women and children, who were supposedly lost, were there, safe and sound. They were on the opposite side of the river and The leaders found a shallow spot and led them back to the cave. The whole colony was now back and greeted them with cheers and hugs.

They unpacked again and stayed for the night, and what a night of celebration it was. Comptes and Navitona gathered all around the ritual campfire. Comptes and Navitona arranged them in circles around the fire. Comptes lifted his hands to the sky and prayed, just as he did when his son was born. He led them in a prayer of thank and Comptes prayed thus, "Oh Greatness! Oh Giver of Life! Oh Thou who has shown mercy to us and has saved the loved ones of our families   this very light order, we thank you! May You be with us and may we be worthy of Thy Presence!" They all began chanting and mumbling sounds that only the Greatness from above could understand. Soon Kibling and others began playing there musical instruments the colony danced for joy to the Lord of the Highest.
That night, Trolldar was in close contact with them and knew that even the Highest Being of the Universe would be pleased with this setting.

The next morning everybody was excited to get packed and head up the trail. They left, at first, leery of what the storm had done to the trail. It was good that they were cautious, for the trail was strewn with debris from the storm. It was hard going for many to maneuver in this twisted mess. The stronger hunters helped them across these places. Then they came across places that were washed out and they had to stop while crews filled in paths big enough for them to cross. Finally, after much extra effort, they made it back to the three canyon open area. They rested as Comptes and Kuballar left to search for the right trail that would lead them over the last mountain pass to the Promised Land.

Comptes led the way and searched the sides of the trail for markers they had left. Comptes went deep into the thicket searching and Kuballar, seeing his earnest search, remarked, "Comptes, are you sure you put them here? Maybe you placed them further up." Comptes was almost angry at his remark, for he knew he never was wrong. He retorted to Kuballar, "No! No! You are wrong there. I know I placed them here, come help me find them." So Kuballar, reluctantly, went into the thicket with Comptes and searched. It didn't take long at all and Kuballar yelled, "Hey, Comptes, over here! I think I found it." Comptes rushed over and sure enough, there it was, The triangle pile of rocks and four rocks in a line pointing up the trail. "You were right as always, so why did I question you," replied Kuballar. Comptes looked around and said, " You know, there is a lot of growth here since we were here last, we must be careful up the trail or we will never find the other markers." Kuballar looked around at all the growth and replied, "You are right there! But that is not all, it is so thick that I am afraid we will have to send a crew ahead, to chop a new trail for the colony to get through. What say, we go back and discuss this and get their input?" "That's a good idea," replied Comptes, "it seems the more we let them have a say in the planning, the more content they are."

All the leaders were getting more excited, now that they were nearing their destination. They were eager to hear every detail of the Adventurers plans. As soon as they heard that Kuballar had called a meeting, so they came running, anxious to hear what Kuballar would tell them. He stepped in front of the group and said, "Men, when we were up on the trail, we found the trail marker but we also found a problem that you have to help us solve. The trail up the mountain pass has changed a great deal since we were here the last time. The heavy rains have

AGE OF ICE

caused the buckastikas and grostiks to become very thick. All the mura grostiks have grown so thick that it is hard even to find a trail. I fear, that many of our people will not be able to travel in this thicket. I called you here so that together we can find a solution to this problem."

The leaders broke up into smaller groups and discussed this new situation. Ohnik was in the same group as Philcor. It didn't take long and they felt that they had come up with an excellent solution to their problem. Ohnik turned to the other groups and shouted, "Men, come together." they gathered back to where they were originally and Ohnik continued, "Philcor and I have discovered a solution that, we think, you all will like. Our plan is simple but should prove a perfect solution. Since Philcor has invented and perfected the axe, we have used it in countless ways. It has become the most versatile tool we have. This same tool will work here. Philcor and his trained men will take their axes up the trail and chop a wide enough path for all of us to travel. He figures that it will take them about three time sets to clear a path to the summit.

This seemed plausible to most and they worked out a detailed plan. The axe men would leave as soon as they got all their tools and supplies ready. The colony would camp here for two time sets while the hunters would replenish the food supply. The remaining leaders and hunters would help set up and maintain the campsite for the next two and one half days. Kuballar set up a special party to help the axe men's families, while they were away.

It was still early afternoon when Philcor and his axe men left. Comptes went a distance with them, to show them the correct trail. Ohnik gathered the best hunters and left to find food for the colony. The game was far more plentiful here in this warm climate. With all the forests, lush vegetation, and abundance of foods, there were many more varieties of different animal then they had ever seen before.

AGE OF ICE

However, they soon found out that it was more difficult to catch these creatures. They were smaller, faster, and had a lot more cover in which to hide. They returned the first day with little to show for their hunt.

That night around the fire they discussed their disappointment with the colony. Everyone seemed to have an answer to their problem but not one, seemed plausible. Then, from the crowd that had gathered around the fire, a young man spoke out, ever so quiet, "Maybe my father could help you. He is very good at finding solutions to difficult tasks." Ohnik got up, pounded his fist against his head and said, "Now why didn't I think of that? Of course, Arteson, your father, Kibling is very talented and clever. He is always coming up with new ideas to solve the most difficult problems." Ohnik went over to where Kibling was sitting by the fire and asked him, Kibling, my good friend, we would be honored if you would accompany us this nusea hence." Kibling stood up and almost was blushing when he spoke, "Why I'd be honored to go with you if you think that I can help."

The hunters left the next morning with Kibling watching their hunting tactics and the animals movements of escape. Sure enough, it didn't take long into the hunt and he had a number of good solutions. First, for the little fast animals that scurried swiftly across the ground, he set up a snare. He bent soft and pliable branches into a loop. He tied a slip tie on one end and slipped another very springy branch through it he placed the loop in the animal's pathway. Kibling then bent the springy branch down under a stick so that when the charging animal steps on the loop, the bent stick sprung up and the loop tightened around the animal's neck, catching it and flinging it up. They tried it and it worked almost every time. Ohnik was so ecstatic at Kibling's snare, that he grabbed him and hugged him "My boy," he cried, "you are greater than the greatest in all of the Age of Icemen."

AGE OF ICE

For the curious and slower animals he created a box by tying sticks crisscross to each other. He put a door on one end and set food inside with a triggered latch that would close the door when the animal went in and picked up the food. On the first try it did not work right and the animal got away. Kibling studied it and made some adjustments. The second try worked and all the others after. They came home that day with an ample supply of food.

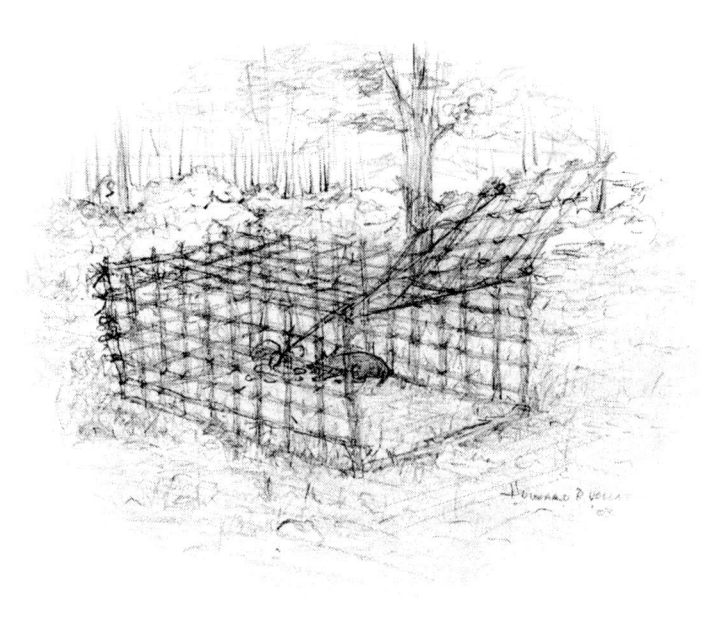

The next day of the hunt Kibling concentrated on making something to catch bigger game. He discovered the idea for this one as he watched some monkey like animals swing through the trees on vines. He quickly cut a number of vines down from the trees and showed some hunters how to help cut them into strip like ropes. He tied them together in a crisscross fashion, creating a net like contraption. It was about three lengths each way. He hung

THE AGE OF ICE

it above the animals pathway and tied the four corners to ropes that he pulled into the thicket. He had one hunter on each rope and when the animal passed under the net, he gave the signal. All four men pulled on their ropes at the same time, the net unloosened from the trees above, the net came crashing down, and the animal was trapped. This too worked most of the time, but sometimes, the hunters were not quick or coordinated enough and the net fell aimlessly to the ground, leaving the animal scurrying away for its life. They divided into groups and each used a different type of Kibling's traps. That day they came home with an abundance of prey that they cleaned, stripped and set aside for curing in the morning.

Around the fire the older hunters told many stories of their past hunts. Some of the day's hunt. Then they all praises turned to Kibling's greatness of thought. Some members devised a song of sorts that went, "Kibling good! He's the one! He be great! He be great! Kibling Butah Mongo! Upah Wishuga! Upah Wishuga! They shouted in a sing-song manner, as they danced around the ritual fire.

On the second day, Philcor and his men were half way up the mountain side. By the third day they reached the summit. Here, they cut a large clearing for the colony to camp when they arrived. In the colony camp, the men gathered to prepare and salt the meat for the remaining journey over the mountain. On the third morning they set out on the trail that Philcor and his men had cleared. Even with the clearing of the thicket, it wasn't easy for some. There were still stumps and roughness on the trail. Some of the young ones and older people, stumbled and fell, cutting and scratching themselves. Soothsay and his aids were busy fixing the wounded and patching up scraps and bruises. They arrived that afternoon to the open arms of Philcor and the other axe men. All were tired for the going wasn't easy so they skipped the ceremonial fire ritual and went straight to bed.

CHAPTER FIFTEEN:
GEO-MAGNETIC FORCES * SADNESS MIXED WITH JOY

While they set up camp, Comptes led the leaders to the edge of the cliff, where they could see their new home. He pointed down to the valley below and said, "There is the Promised Land, just as the Adventurers said it would be. They looked and stared at the awesome sight. There was nothing but lush forest and prairie, filled with grasses and flowering bushes. Comptes and Navitona raised their hands to the sky and said, "Men, this is a momentous occasion that we all have been waiting for. Butah Mongo, the great one from above has watched over us and brought us our Promised Land, now it is up to us to thank and praise him." They all folded their hands and bowed in reverence, as Comptes began, "Oh Butah Mongo, the Great One from above, we thank you and praise you for keeping us safe. As we arrive at our Promised Land, let us live lives that are fitting to thee." The leaders started to chant, "Butah Mongo! Butah Mongo!" It was becoming evident that Comptes and his son were becoming the colonies spiritual leaders. Comptes and Kuballar went over the next few days plans. Ohnik turned to the Adventurers and said, "Some were skeptical but now we know. It is good! You were more than right to tell us to journey here. We will all be thankful to you and your names will be remembered on the lips of all our people." The leaders were so touched by Ohnik's remarks, that they joined in with Upah Mongo! Upah Mongo! After all were through admiring their new land, they went back to camp and spread the joyous news of what they had just seen. That night they had reason to celebrate and celebrate they did. The joy spread throughout the entire camp and some were so caught up by the emotions of the moment, that they ventured off into the forest, for their own private party.

While the colony waited at the summit, Philcor and his men were really getting adept at using their

AGE OF ICE

axes. What took previously two days, now they accomplished in one. They were already at the half way point and making good time, when suddenly, the earth opened up and tons of rocks started flying upwards. They flew straight up to a higher outcropping ledge and became apart of that ledge. The team of men that were working there were lucky. Only a few were knocked down and bruised from the flying boulders. Philcor and the men on his team came dashing over to see what happened. Just as they were approaching, the same mass of rocks, came tumbling back down into the hole they came from. The dust settled and the ground around it looked almost undisturbed. Luckily again, Philcor and his team were well enough away from the boulders to cause them any harm. Philcor looked around to check if all his men were alright. The ones nearest the hole, got up and brushed themselves off. Only two had bruises. Some others, farther away, were still standing but just stood there in shock. Then he heard some cries and moans from below the edge of the trail. Philcor ran over and there lay four of his men, about ten lengths down and up against some brush and trees. When the explosion hit, the force was so great, that it knocked them off their feet and down this steep embankment and they tumbled up against the brush and trees. Philcor called down to them, "Are you alright down there?" One of them replied, "I am but I think the others are hurt." Philcor had learned to make rope from Kibling and quickly he got some of the men to help him strip and weave a rope long enough to reach the men below. Philcor threw the rope down to them and the one that was alright, tied the rope to the most injured one, and they carefully pulled him up. They laid him on a soft skin and let the rope down again. The other three yelled up that they were alright so they used the rope to help them climb the steep embankment. Philcor checked them over as well and the one that was slightly bruised said, "Man, are we lucky. Those rocks came exploding out of the ground like some monster. We didn't have time to get out of the way. The boulders hit us with such

AGE OF ICE

force, that we tumbled way down below, where you found us. The other one added, "Yes, that was wild and mad. What kind of evil is this?" Philcor just kind of looked blank as he replied, "I really haven't an answer for that question. But, when we get back, all of us must tell our stories to the leaders." They then attended the more injured man. Soothsay had sent along some healing salves and taught one of the axe men how to prepare a wound properly. When he seemed well enough they made a bed of skins in a little cove for him to rest while they finished clearing the trail. They made a detour far around the force field so as not to entangle the colony in that monster.

Jealon had also taken a crew along with Philcor's axe men. He was the most gifted in finding and identifying caves. After Philcor had reached the bottom of the mountain trail, it would be the job of Jealon and his men to find as many suitable caves as needed for the families of the colony. It took Philcor just one day to finish the trail to the opening at the bottom of the forest that gradually led down to the valley below. Philcor camped that night with Jealon and bright and early, he was off to pick up his wounded axe man and carry him back to the colony, where Soothsay could heal him properly. As they left, Jealon gave Philcor, strict instructions, to be sure to keep the colony up on the mountain pass for at least two days, before they started down the trail. He knew it would take at least that long to find suitable caves for all the families. Philcor assured him that he would and he said, as he parted, "My wounded man may need at least that much time or even longer, for him to heal. I will tell the leaders what you said." With that, they gave the ritual salute, then, Philcor and his many men disappeared up the trail.

Jealon and his crew cut a trail through the remaining forest and into the valley below. As they chopped the last remaining obstacle, they were confronted with a sight they could hardly believe.

AGE OF ICE

Jealon raised his hands in praise and said "Glory to the Greatness above, for this is a sight greater than my eyes have ever seen. Thanks be to Thee, Oh Butah Mongo!" and all his men chanted, "Butah Mongo! Butah Mongo!" What a sight to behold. Spacious fields of grasses, plants, and flowers. In all directions, they could see clumps of bushes and trees as far as the eye could carry. "Look men," shouted Jealon, exuberant, "this is the Promised Land, this is our new home. "After a long while of taking in all the beauty and giving thanks, Jealon turned to his men and said, "If we are going to find enough caves for all our people, we had better get started."

Jealon led them out into the valley so they could get a better look at the terrain. They discussed different plans together and the Jealon said," Let us travel along the mountain edges. We will divide into searching groups so we can find more caves in a shorter period of time. We will go up and down the mountain's edges. If you find a cave, blow your warning horn. We will all meet back here at nusea down."

Off they went in all directions, eager to set up their new home. Jealon found the first cave. He stopped just short of a familiar looking outcrop and studied it for a minute. "Sure enough," he thought, "it looks exactly like the ones in Feriandimal." He then asked his assistant, "Look, Ubcar, "isn't that the same rock forms, where large caves are in, back in Feriandimal?" Ubcar looked at where he was pointing and then replied, "Why yes, that sure looks the same to me." "Come, let us find the opening of the cave."

It was not as easy as Jealon had hoped. When he got close to the ridge, there was a steep out crop that they had to travel around. They had to crawl under it and clear a lot of debris away. When they finally crawled to the end, they found no entrance. Jealon was now frustrated and almost used profane

AGE OF ICE

language, when he yelled out, "By butsakuf, I know my caves and there has got to be one here!" Ubcar looked surprised at Jealon for he usually never got upset. He was always noted for his level headed and precise thoughts. But, this is exactly why he got mad. For the first time he was stumped. Then, Ubcar replied to him, "You are my mentor and I believe in you. If you say a cave is here, then it is!"

Jealon was pleased with his response and became settled down to his normal thinking process. Then, he got an idea and said to Ubcar, "Look there, at those boulders that are sticking out from the wall. Let us dig and move these obstructions from the wall and I bet, we'll find the opening." They used their axes as shovels to remove the loose sand and gravel, then they took their spears and pried the larger boulders out of their moorings. They got a couple of big ones out of the way and there, they saw the dark outlines of an entrance. Now, they dug with careless fervor and as they rattled and twisted their spears and threw rocks and boulders away from the opening, suddenly, it released tons of rocks and boulders from above. The rocks came crashing down behind them, missing them by just inches. They were huddled together against the wall and when the dust settled, turned and looked up. To their surprise, instead of a calamity and failure, it looked like a miracle. The rock slide had just removed all the rocks covering the opening and there before them, was a large opening to the cave. But above, unbeknownst to them, was their protectorate , Trolldar, the Wizard of the Mountain Trails. It was no accident, but rather, a wizard's hands who guided the rocks away from them safely. He was smiling, for it came out even better than Trolldar even planned.

Jealon, seeing the large opening to the cave, hugged Ubcar and rejoiced with him in celebration. He took out the horn and was the first one to signal the sound of victory. Each of the other search parties, stopped and threw up their arms in the

AGE OF ICE

traditional salute for his success. Jealon and Ubcar made up some torches, soaked them with oil from their packs and lit them. They entered the cave and searched its various parts. There were many small shafts going back into the mountain. In a couple of places they had to crawl to get through but one of the shafts, they could see an opening that led to a large room. Some boulders and smaller rocks had fallen in the doorway. As they were clearing them away, they heard some angry growling and snarling noises deep inside the chamber. They quickly took their spears, backed up and waited. As waited, they peered into the darkness to where they heard the noise. In the far corner there appeared to be two shiny eyes glistening in the reflection of the torch light. Jealon whispered lowly to Ubcar, "We must be very careful, for we know not what kind of animals live in these parts. They slowly crept forward to get a glimpse of its outline but stayed back out of its danger zone. "That sure enough looks like that hoolik beast we have back in Feriandimal." Ubcar stared at it also and said, "It looks like your right, and I think I see more than two eyes shining. If these are hooliks , we sure don't want to fool with him by ourselves." "You're sure right there, Ubcar. Those beasts are really mean. We had better leave them alone and let the colony hunters get them."

Just as they came out of the cave, they heard another horn blow. "Ah Ubcar," rejoiced Jealon, "another cave is found." They left and went up the ridge to a lower dry river bed to search for another.

It was Ohnik's cousin, Pitil and his assistant, who found the second cave. He also was a student of Jealon and followed his every word and skill. He was exact in following the rock structures as Jealon told him. He learned that many caves are located near river bottoms. He saw this river bank, that he was following, led into a small canyon. There, it flowed right into and through the wall of

AGE OF ICE

the mountain. He and his assistant had to pry rocks away to find the opening. they were headed just down stream from the first cave and came across another. Again, he blew the horn and was one ahead of his mentor, but it didn't take long for Jealon to catch up, as he too blew the horn a second time. Late that afternoon, The other search party found a cave as well. They all saw the sun receding in the sky and headed back to camp.

They talked about their successes and where each one was. Then Jealon told them about the hooliks in the first cave. After they ate they sat around the fire and planned the next day's search. Each gave a different idea as to how to find the next caves. After even some calling each others ideas dumb, Jealon interrupted them and said, It seems like we will never come up with a plan this way. I have the best success and taught many of you the skills you have, so I will take it upon myself to tell you exactly how we are going to do it tomorrow." There was all quiet now as he spoke for they realized their folly. Jealon continued, "my plan is to venture farther out into the valley flatlands. in the center there is a hill that we can climb up on. From there, we can see the entire structures of the mountain ridges and river flows." They all talked his plan over and agreed that he was , again way ahead of them. Jealon continued, "Nusea hence we will take one group upways and one group downways," as he pointed in their directions, "and remember to blow your horns when you find a cave."

The next morning they followed Jealon out to the valley floor. At first the going was smooth. Their were animal paths between the bushes and grass. Farther out the grass was almost hip high and it made the walking more difficult. When they neared the hill it became more rocky and barren, which made it easier to travel. Once they arrived at the top of the hill, they could see the contours of the mountains and plan their routes of exploration. They studied paths where finding caves looked best.

AGE OF ICE

Jealon and his crew didn't leave the valley right away. They explored the various upper sections in it and found berries and many fragrant flowers. They lazily headed toward their goal of various river beds downside. That day Jealon blew his horn three times. The other group as well blew their horn many times. By evening around the fire place, they counted their finds and found that they had discovered two hands and two fingers of caves. Jealon counted the caves and the families and reported that they still should find at least one more day of caves." "Men, tomorrow we will each go further. I will take my men further upwards and you, Pitil, take your crew futher downwards.

Kuballar stood before the entire gathering of the colony. He got up on a tall edge and addressed them, "The days of waiting are almost over. Philcor tells us that we must give the cave hunters one more day. So it will be soon when we journey forth to our Promised Land. There will be beauty beyond belief. You heard the report from Philcor and I am sure by now that Jealon will have plenty of homes for you when you arrive. But I must warn you, Philcor also told us of a mountain trail, vicious rock explosion. We must be extra careful in our journey through that site. Plan that each family can watch out for danger and warn each other. So, spend the day dreaming of your new home and we will contact all of you tomorrow." Even with the day delay and the news of the rock explosion, the colony's enthusiasm did not diminish, in fact it expanded. That night there was an exuberance of singing, dancing, blowing horns, and again, some couples sneaking off into the deeper part of the woods.

Ohnik was up before the women had even started the morning meal. He and Philcor met with Kuballar, Comptes, Pillas, and Kibling. His mind was reeling all night over those rocks. "How could those rocks force their way up out of the earth and then disappeared again into the earth?" As these thoughts

AGE OF ICE

kept coming and coming. He wanted a conference to discuss this before they left and to relieve his mind. They talked for hours as to what it could be. Pillas said that his body was sensing danger and they should be extra careful. Philcor assured them that he marked the place carefully and cut a path far enough around to avoid contact with it. Ohnik felt satisfied and gathered the colony to announce their departure that very morning.

On their departure some were so excited that they left some of their belongings behind and they had to backtrack. It was a good thing they did, for when they got back, they found one members child, sitting in the middle of the belongings, crying her heart out.

Once underway, the journey down started out to be a breeze compared to other days on the trail. It was even easy stepping over the stumps left behind by Philcor's axe men. But not all turned out so also enjoyable. Half way down the mountain path it clouded up and soon, it began pouring. Then heavy winds blew in and caused the rain to feel like knives on their faces. The weather turned unusually cold and they had to stop and put on heavier clothing. They also were approaching the force field rock area. Philcor showed Comptes where the force field was and they routed the colony around on the newly cut trail. The detour trail wasn't as flat as the other and the path angled sideways and had higher stumps. The heavy rain was also making the path very slippery and slimy. It was now becoming very treacherous to even navigate at all on this trail.

They stopped for a moment to discuss their dilemma and what to do about it, when suddenly, a bolt of lightning came crashing down. It hit a huge tree, splintering it and causing it to come crashing down across the trail in front of them. Many of the colony members panicked as they jumped when startled by the tree. They lost their balance and slid over

AGE OF ICE

the embankment and down the slimy, muddy slope. Luckily there were enough trees and bushes below to catch their fall, for just below them was a canyon with cliffs that went straight down four hundred feet.

The Adventurers and other leaders came running to where they had slid down the mountain slope. They looked down and saw them stranded by the trees below. It was too slippery for any of them to go down and pull them up. Quickly, Kuballar went into action. Through the pouring sheets of rain, he yelled orders to the men, "The vines! Cut all the vines you can find." They didn't understand why but did as he said.
"Now, let us form teams and each of our teams tie the vines together so they will reach the people below. Tie one of you to the vines and the other stronger men let him down. Pick up the wounded first and pull them up. Then the rest. The rest of us will go back to where the other colony members are and keep them safe." They quickly went into action and tied the vines together, tied the rescuers on them and lowered them down to the victims below. Pillas had gone down first and brought up a wounded woman. He reported the conditions and sent others down to bring up other wounded people. Soothe say tried to bind her wounds but the mud and wetness was too great. He decided just to clean the wounds and stop the blood flow. Then when it let up dress the wounds properly.

The leaders saw that Kuballar's rescue method was working and started back up to where the other colony people were. Pillas had also finished concentrating on the wounded below and was about to join Kuballar and go up the hill when a sudden danger signal raced through his body. He turned and scampered up the hill as fast as he could. But it was too late, for suddenly, the force field opened up and started its thunderous roaring of rocks that flew out of the hole and up to the cliff above. With the turmoil all around them some of the member

AGE OF ICE

forgot about Philcor's warning markers and ventured too close to the force field. As it opened its gapping mouth some of the members fell in and got thrown upwards with the thundering and pounding rocks, to be crushed on top and flung like sacks to the ground. Others slipped and fell in later and got buried as the thunderous, flying rocks came crashing back into its hole. Pillas seeing this tragedy before his eyes, rent his vest and pounded his chest in agony bewailing the fact that he didn't have time to warn them. when the leaders got close they counted over fifteen mutilated bodies lying in every direction from the force field. Some were in parts, torn by the force of the flying rocks. Those that were eaten by the force field would never be found and they had no idea how many. When Trolldar arrived at the scene he too knew that this might was beyond his powers and his abilities to have helped.

That night the rains let up and the moon shone through the trees, glimmering sparkles of hope down upon the colony. In the morning it was time to mend the wounded, first, then bury the dead that they could gather together. Comptes and Navitona had a solemn ceremony to honor their loved ones. He prayed for the ones they buried and the ones they couldn't find. It took the a day and one half but they were on their last leg of a long journey home.

Jealon and Ubcar had found all the caves necessary for all the colony families. When the colony did not arrive on the expected day, they went out and found two more extra caves. Some of the men also went on a hunt so there would be fresh meat for the arrival of the colony.

The colony was a day and one half late when Jealon finally saw them coming down the trail and into the open valley of their new home. He expected to hear cheers of joy and shouts of amazement from the on coming voyagers, but what he saw was sad faces, injured people and some still mourning their dead.

AGE OF ICE

Comptes saw that Jealon was in shock at what he saw and took him aside and filled him in on the tragedy. "Luckily though," Comptes said, "half of the colony had slipped down the slippery slope and was spared a tragic death with the quick thinking of Kuballar. He had us tie vines together and rescue all the people trapped, down on the slope below. Only a few got cuts and bruises that Soothsay mended.

AGE OF ICE

Their was not much celebrating in camp that night, even though they waited many nuseas and nooma reflects to get here. Rather, Comptes and Navitona led them in a solemn prayer session that lasted late into the night. They led the vigil around the traditional fire circle and prayed thanks for how many were rescued from the terrible tragedy, and most of all for leading them to their home, the Promised Land.

In the morning the sadness had subsided and some even celebrated their new home. The leaders took many families around and showed them the many wonders of their new home. Jealon and Ubcar led them around and showed them all the caves they had found. The hunters made short work of the hooliks in the cave. The leaders directed the families in choosing the proper caves for each family or family group. All again seemed happy and content in their new environment.

Finally, after many nuseas, and many nooma reflects, they were at peace and in harmony with their surroundings. They could live, for the first time in the Age of Icemen, without worry of peril, lack of food, being eaten by a monster predator, or freezing to death, caught in a glacier. "Yes," announced Ohnik to every one as he stood before the Adventurers, "These young men truly are our heroes. They have given us more than we ever dreamed possible. Yes, my friends, Their names will be on the lips of all generations to follow." The Colony in unison shouted, Upah Wishuga! Butah Mongo!" They shouted this over and over as they danced around the fire. Then, as they danced, Kuballar spoke with a loud voice declaring, "Let it be known here and in the future that we shall no longer be called, Age of Icemen. Our name henceforth shall be, the New Age People of Mittebyro." It was the future that held the most promise for them for they would be the leaders and bring the Age of Icemen into a new era of growth, development, and cultural advancements even they never dreamed possible.

APPENDIX A: NAMES OF PEOPLE

1) OHNIK & WIFE, RENEDO
2) JONCAR & WIFE, BONESTRA
3) JEALON & WIFE MOVENEA
4) PHILCOR & WIFE, ESTRA
5) KUBALLAR
6) KIBLING & WIFE, BENTRA
7) COMPTES & WIFE, CELESTRA
8) PILLAS & WIFE, SENSORA
9) WHORMWICK
10) ARTESON & WIFE PENTIMA
11) NAVITONA
12) SOOTHSAY & WIFE COMFEREA
13),14),15) OXENYA, QUESTOMA, & OHPEHA
16),17) UBCAR & PITIL
18) OUSPA
19) TROLLDAR
20) DO-O-MAGNICENT - DOOMAGNON

APPENDIX A: FACTS ABOUT PEOPLE

OHNIK & WIFE RENEDO   HIGHEST ELDER LEADER

Ohnik was respected and feared by all who knew him in Feriandimal. He had exceptional hunting skills and the other hunters looked up to him for advice. He eventually became leader of the Council of Hunters. He was the first person Do-o-magnicent sought out to touch the glowing Ball of Knowledge. The change in his life revolutionized the entire Age of Ice community. Touching the ball transformed him into a man who suddenly understood that wisdom and love was a better choice than anger and force. When his son and the other Adventurers returned with their fantastic tales, Ohnik convinced most of the Hunter Council's families to travel with him to find this Promised Land.

Renedo was the first women to take charge and organize all the families and the domestic job assignments of the colony as they journeyed to the Promised Land. Ohnik appointed her head director caves, families, and domestics.

JONCAR & WIFE BONESTRA   OLDEST OF THE ELDER LEADERS

As Joncar aged in life he discovered secrets of finding trail, He became the wisest and most revered trail leader in the Council of Hunters. He was appointed trail leader in the colonies journey to the Promised Land. He led the colony until he ran past his familiar hunting grounds, then he turned the leadership over to the Adventurers. His most important contribution to the colony was the sacrificing of his life when he helped kill the two headed fire dragon.

Bonestra, helped Renedo organize and maintain the families in the caves and cared for the young.

APPENDIX A: FACTS ABOUT PEOPLE

JEALON & WIFE MOVENA, ELDER LEADER & MEDIATOR

Jealon was a close friend of Ohnik. In their many hunting trips, Ohnik recognized Jealon's talents in finding caves. Ohnik appointed his friend to be the leader cave finding during their journey. He also was, captain in charge, in the advanced party into the promised land. There, he and his crew found all the caves for the entire colony. His wife Movenea was gifted in helping Soothsay with the wounded people along the journey.

PHILCOR & WIFE ESTRA, STRONGEST ELDER LEADER

Philcor was the youngest and the strongest of the elder leaders. After his encounter with the Glowing Ball of Knowledge, he became very inventive, creating an advanced axe and training many how to use it effectively.

Estra, also contributed to helping other women adjust to the colony trail. She helped Soothsay with his healing on the trail.

KUBALLAR & WIFE KISTRA

Kuballar, first born son of Ohnik, was given the Glowing Ball of Knowledge. This gave him new insights for adventurer and he became one of the four Adventurers who found the Promised Land. He convinced his father to lead the colony of Age of Icemen, from Feriandimal to the newly discovered land. He was a born leader and became the head leader of the New Age Mittebyro.

KIBLING first born son of Joncar, and became an elder leader when his father met his death at the hands of the two headed fire dragon. Kuballar passed the Glowing Ball of Knowledge to him and he

APPENDIX A: FACTS ABOUT PEOPLE

immediately wanted to join the Adventurers in exploring new lands. He also gained an extra ordinary talent to see the world around him and record it as cave art.

COMPTES PONTIFF HIGH ORDERLINESS I & WIFE CELESTRA

Comptes, first born of Jealon, was not prominent in the beginning of the colonies journey. Kibling passed the glowing ball to Comptes and he gained a strong sense of direction and an insight into religion. He was one of the four Adventurers and they owe their success to his uncanny sense of direction and his ability to memorize land marks. He learned to navigate, using the stars for direction. Later, he became very religious with the birth of his new born son on the trail.

PILLAS & WIFE SENSORA

Pillas, first born son of Philcor, was introduced to the Glowing Ball of Knowledge by Comptes. He always had the ability to sense danger but now it became his intuitions became ten times more sensitive. He not only could sense danger, but knew way before it was about to happen and could warn everybody to avoid it. He became one of the adventurers and saved their lives on many an occasion. Although some of the colony lost their lives on the journey, Pillas helped many in his ability to sense danger. He was one of the key participants in the slaying of the fire dragons, alerting the hunters of both the dragons. Sensora was a women who inspired her children to seek after the greatness of Pillas and their grandfather, Philcor.

WHORMWICK was grandson of Ohnik, first born son of Kuballar, learned all his traits of leadership watching his father and grandfather in action.

APPENDIX A: FACTS ABOUT PEOPLE

ARTESON & WIFE PENTIMA

Arteson, grandson of Joncar, first born son of Kibling, journeyed with his father from Feriandimal to the Promised Land. He helped his father carve and paint the pictures in the caves, as they journeyed with the colony.

NAVITONA, HIGH MONSENIOR & TEACHER

Navitona, grandson of Jealon, oldest son of Comptes, and heir to the priesthood. He did not marry, but instead, devoted his life to spiritual insights that he first learned on the trail.

SOOTHSAY, ELDER HUNTER & HEALER

Soothsay was one of the original Age of Icemen who journeyed to the Promised Land. When he was hunting in Feriandimal, he became interested in a few plants that survived the sub-zero frigid weather. He found that, not only were they eatable, but some, could heal wounds and cure sicknesses. He applied these new herbs on the colony's journey to their new land and became respected as a healer among all the people. As he journeyed down the various trails, he found the same herbs and some surprising new ones. He added these to his collection and found even more cures and healing processes.

OXENYA, ELDER HUNTER & DISSENTER, WIFE HISTRA

Oxenya was one of the original Age of Icemen who journeyed with Ohnik to the Promised Land. Although he was a good hunter, he never led any hunting parties, later, became a bitter dissenter. He became

APPENDIX A: FACTS ABOUT PEOPLE

known throughout the colony for his abstinent composure. He questioned almost every leaders comments, orders, or directives. He would try to sway the majority to rebel against their leaders. If the majority of the colony went along with their leaders and, only after much dialogue, would he reluctantly accept the leader's commands.

QUESTOMA, ELDER HUNTER\PEACEMAKER & WIFE, GENSEA

Questoma was a good hunter in Feriandimal. He was well liked by the leaders and his peers as well. Although he too questioned the leaders, when the colony traveled from Feriandimal to the Promised Land, Questoma was very helpful in quieting the various dissenters. He even changed many of their minds into turning around and returning to Feriandimal. His wife was very useful in all activities and helped Renedo in preparing all the caves.

OHPEHA, ELDER HUNTER\PEACEMAKER & WIFE MIDA

Ohpeya and Questoma were close friends. They thought and greed alike on most subjects. When problems arose in the colony and Questoma could not quell the anger, then Ohpeya came to the rescue. He even gave the dissenters new insights and respect for the Adventurers. He along with Questoma, prevented many of the colony from turning back in their journey. His wife Mida helped Soothsay with the birth of Comptes's son.

UBCAR & PITEL

Ubcar had always admired Jealon's ability to find caves. He quickly volunteered to be his assistant when the cave hunting party went ahead to find cave for everyone in the Promised Land.

APPENDIX A: FACTS ABOUT PEOPLE

Pitil was a cousin of Ohnik and good in his own right in finding caves. He was assigned as second leader in search of caves in the new land.

OUSPA

Ouspa, son of Oxenya, was the most cunning of all the cave dweller killers. He had an outstanding ability to track and sneak up on his prey without being seen or heard. He grew up listening to his father's dissenting questions and became cynical himself. He felt he was a better hunter than Ohnik but no one paid attention to him.

TROLLDAR, WIZARD OF THE MOUNTAIN TRAILS

Trolldar grew up learning all the wisdom and knowledge of the Middle Spirit World. His mother acquired the renowned High Wizard, Mariandimith. He was the leading teacher of all wizards in the Middle Spirit World. He taught Trolldar all the illusionary tricks, conjuration, his secret magical formulas, and sorcery spells. He became a wizard of the highest order. Son of Gomingan and Questare, he had only himself to blame if he did not succeed. He did not fail them and exceeded even their greatness. Word of his success spread throughout the galaxies. Soon, he was invited to attend a spiritual Transformation Seminar held by invitation only at the Spiritual Quandactories of his old instructor, Mariandimith. While attending he exceeded all expectations, so Mariandimith immediately placed him in an advanced school, where he learned many exceptional forms of magic, and most important aspect of his training, the power to train ones mind and body to appear transparent. He was awarded the highest honor and title of High Wizard Quandactor Transparent, but he kept this a secret and revealed it only to his most closest associates.

APPENDIX A: FACTS ABOUT PEOPLE

Trolldar was assigned to watch and protect the colony on their journey to the Promised Land. He secretly followed them on the trail and intervened when danger overwhelmed the members of the colony.

DO-O-MAGNICENT\DOOMAGNON A WIZARD TURNED EVIL

It was not known exactly where Doomagnon actually came from in his youth, all he remembers is a great war between many planets. Doomagnon's planet was destroyed along with his parents and all that they possessed. He was taken in by a great leader who rescued many from this devastation. His name was Omaran The Great and his heroism and courage was spread far and wide. Omaran took Doomagnon in and raised him as his own son. When he arrived he could not understand what the boy's real name was originally, so he gave him the name, Doomagnon. Omaran taught him all he knew but realized this exceptional boy needed more, but it was something that he could not give him. When the wars diminished and peace came to these parts, Theasium took it upon himself to reward those that stayed true to the faith and fought till freedom was restored. While Theasium was traveling throughout the kingdoms, he came to meet with Omaran and reward him for his heroism. After the ceremonies, Omaran spoke to Theasium about Doomagnon, saying, "This boy is very bright and has already absorbed all that I have to give him. There are many times that I have watched him wonder off into the hills and stare out into space. I fear, that between his high intelligence and his great losses, I will not be able to help him. Theasium took the boy aside and spent some time with him, drilling him and asking many advanced questions. After the session was over, Theasium returned to Omaran and said, "This boy is an exceptionally gifted individual and I shall see

APPENDIX A: FACTS ABOUT PEOPLE

what I can do to help him. I must still attend other award ceremonies but I will return and give you my answer. I will take the boy with me for further observation." As Theasium was leaving, Omaran bowed and thanked him.

Theasium did indeed find the boy to be exceptional as Omaran had said, so when he returned from his journeys with Doomagnon, he gave Omaran his decision. "Omaran", said Theasium, "you have done wonders with this boy and I bless you for taking him in as your own son, but now it is time for this lad to learn more and take advantage of his gifts. Pack up all of Doomagnon's possessions. I have one more errand to run and when I return I will take him with me." "Oh blessed be Your Greatness," replied Omaran, "you have filled our whole land with joy and happiness."

Theasium took Doomagnon to the High Council of Wizards and asked that they appoint a number of wizards to train him. Theasium spoke to them saying, "I want this young man to learn all that he must know in order to become one of the great wizards of the galaxies and perhaps even a member of the High Council of Wizards." They conferred together in council and returned and the leader spoke, "We have chosen three of the best wizards to fulfill your request, for it is an honor and privilege to serve you in this manner, Your Greatness" They all bowed as Theasium departed, knowing that he had left Doomagnon in capable hands.

He learned fast and became a member of the High Council of Wizards. He eventually became their leader and as he grew in importance and honor his name was changed to Do-o-magnicent.

While Trolldar was assigned the task of watching

APPENDIX A: FACTS ABOUT PEOPLE

over and protecting the colony on the trail, Do-o-magicent was assigned the task of planting the Glowing Ball of Knowledge where the Age of Icemen's leader, Ohnik, could find it and be transformed. He also was assigned the task of watching over their growth and development and that they would eventually meet the level of expectation that Theasium requested. Unfortunately he later falls into temptation and never accomplishes his task.

APPENDIX B: NAMES OF PLACES

1) FERIANDIMAL

2) LOCKNESS SOUTH CAMP

3) MT. DARKNESS

4) MT. DOUBLER

5) TUBRES GORGE

6) MOUNT MORGAN

7) DRAGON KINGDOM

8) BEARROD CANYON

9) BLOOMSCENT VALLEY

10) TOOKSAY NARROWS

11) BICERUS PASS

12) BACARIS CANYON

13) MEGAR FLATS

14) MUCH UPS PASS

15) MUCH OHTS CANYON

16) THE CAVE OF THE THREE CANYONS

17) PROMITHIUS PASS

18) THE TRAIL OF THE PROMISED LAND

APPENDIX B: NAMES OF PLACES

FERIANDIMAL THE AGE OF ICE BEGINNING LAND

Feriandimal was, for all practical purposes, a total series of ice caps with mountains and rock ridges protruding from its openings. Their were little fauna and flora existing, save a few scant bushes and herbs. Even with this sparse environment, many species of living creatures managed to exist. It was this tenacious attitude that enabled these Age of Icemen to exist and eventually get the attention of those higher in the universal chain to come and rescue them from their interlocking demise.

LOCKNESS CAMP OF NUSEA DOWN UNDER

Lockness was the area where Ohnik and all his colony lived before their journey to the Promised Land. It was a more inhabitable environment than the rest of Feriandimal. They also had access to the ocean where they used the salt for curing meat and occasionally catching some fish or sea mammals. It is here, in a cave, that Do-o-magnicent places the Glowing Ball of Knowledge and advances the people to seek a better life.

MT. DARKNESS & MT. DOUBLER lay on either side of the hunting trail that the colony took to their new land. They were the northern most mountains of the entire ridge they passed through. The colony passed through them on a narrow trail where they camped. It was here that the colony was shocked as swordenfin tubres attacked and killed a young boy in the colony and injured a women.

TUBRES GORGE was really slow and treacherous going in this steep, rough, and rocky gorge. All the leaders had to take extra care to see that all the children and old people did not stumble and fall

APPENDIX B: FACTS ABOUT PLACES

on any sharp rocks or fall into one of the many deep crevices. This was a perfect place for the swordenfin tubres to get their revenge. Un known to most of the colony, an entire herd of tubres were following them and waiting for the right moment to attack. Pillas, though, with his inner sensory warning system, alerted the guards far enough in advance to set a counter trap and avoid further bloodshed.

MOUNT MORGAN

Although Ohnik, Jealon, Philcor, and Joncar had hunted in parts of Mount Morgan, it was so steep and rugged that the colony had to pass to one side of it. Even the best of the Age of Icemen had failed to climb to its summit. They chose a flatter and lower trail that went around the mount. It was here that the scenery changed. Gradually the colony saw fewer and fewer ice fields and began to see what the Adventurers called. grostiks. It was also in this same area that the colony encountered the Fire dragons.

DRAGON KINGDOM

The two headed fire dragon, Bibutsakufascorchum, was so powerful and mighty that he set up his own kingdom. Anyone who dared to enter his domain was sure to die a sudden and fiery death. His kingdom was situated just down from Mount Morgan. The colony had to find a way to pass by his kingdom in order to continue their journey.

BEARROD CANYON & BLOOMSCENT VALLEY

The colony spent some time recuperating from the dragon experience and enjoying the warmer weather.

APPENDIX B: NAMES OF PLACES

They pact and traveled through the Bearrod Canyon, camping on its crest. It was the last ruminants of ice. As they journeyed down the canyon they came to, Bloomscent Valley, what some of them described as paradise. It was filled with fragrant flowers of all kinds, bushes with nuts and berries, and large trees with huge canopies.

TOOKSAY NARROWS was as ugly and harsh as Bloomscent Valley was pleasant and beautiful. In every edge of every cliff there were large worms called rubalangers. They were about six inches to a foot long and thirsty for blood. The canyon is so narrow that the worms could strike from each side and hit you. It was the only accessible pass from north to south. The colony had no other choice but to go through it.

BICERUS PASS

The Adventurers had given the colony extra precautions regarding the treachery of the Bicerus Pass. It was rocky, uneven, and unpredictable and so it was as they passed through it. The ground shook and swayed under their feet. Large boulders and rocks broke loose overhead and came tumbling down toward the colony as its slowly snaked its way, cautiously through this treacherous trail. Even before Pillas could react with his super sensing powers, the boulders and rocks crashing down on hordes of colony members. Bicerus Pass again kept its treacherous name alive.

BACARIS CANYON unlike its predecessor, this canyon proved to be an easy trip. It was sturdy with its pathway wide and flat. The colony could also see glimpses of the paradise that lay ahead of them. With all the new warmth and beauty around them, many got caught up in the new emotion of love

APPENDIX B: NAMES OF PLACES

between husbands and wives as they found secluded corners to express themselves to each other. Never had an environment played so heavy on the members of the colony before.

MEGAR FLATS

As the Bacaris Canyon descended, Megar Flats Appeared. It wasn't a disappointment to the colony, for it was pleasant and very inviting to them as they traveled in this flat and warm surroundings. But, the Adventurers had warned them of the perils from the sky, for on their first journey through this paradise, they were attacked by flesh eating beast of the sky that they called armaflorvias.

MUCH UPS PASS

The pass leads the colony to the final leg of their journey. It is here, in a quiet cave, that the first child is born on the journey to the Promised Land. Trolldar is stationed above and takes special notice to these Age of Icemen and how far they have come in accepting the ways of harmony and love. Particularly Comptes, the father, who becomes more aware and closer to the spirituality of those from above.

<u>MUCH OHTS CANYON</u> was the final canyon before they crossed into the Promised Land. It was wide and flat in many spots but got narrow and rocky in others. When it is in the dry season, it is easy and wonderful trek through this canyon. When there are heavy rains, the canyon becomes treacherous as the colony experienced.

THE CAVE OF THE THREE CANYONS

Comptes led the colony safely down the wide canyon

APPENDIX B: NAMES OF PLACES

and into the three canyon entrance. The Adventurers had camped here but there camp was way too small for the colony. Jealon organized a party and found a large enough cave to house the entire colony. It was located just down in the right branch canyon river. This find turned out to be a catastrophe. Unbeknownst to them the cave was not set high enough above the flood plain. Heavy rains descended upon them and filled the cave with water. Many women and children panicked and ran out into the river, only to be swept away by the surging river flow. Only Trolldar, with his magic, saved them from utter chaos.

PROMITHIUS PASS

The adventurers approached this final trail but found it filled with unbelievable undergrowth. It was so thick with vegetation that they even couldn't find their markers. It would be up to Philcor and his axe men to clear a path for the colony. This was not the only stumbling block in Promithius Pass for, when the colony finally found their way through the cleared thicket, a bigger, more dangerous impediment was about to encompass them and take many as their own.

THE TRAIL OF THE PROMISED LAND

Jealon took a crew and cut a final trail to their new land. As the colony descended, they found the trail to widen out and flatten on the last of their journey. To their surprise, it open to a complete view of the Promised Land. Later, the leaders used this trail to get to their secret rendezvous, where they held their ceremonial rituals and some to meditate.

APPENDIX C: NAMES OF ANIMALS & BIRDS

1) SWORDENFIN TUBRES
2) DEMON BEAST
3) KUPABIN
4) BIBUTSAKUFASCORCHUM
5) DAGGER
6) RUBALANGERS
7) ARMAFLORVIA
8) GOULA
9) HOOLIK
10) BORGAMUTH

ARMAFLORVIA

APPENDIX C: FACTS ABOUT ANIMALS & BIRDS

SWORDENFIN TUBRES

The tubres lived mainly in the mountain ice packs of Feriandimal. They were mid-sized and ferocious beasts with extended and sharp canine teeth. They could cut most prey in half with one bite. They were more intelligent than most animals. They were able to communicate between each other with sophisticated sounds and intricate foot tapping. Many an Age of Ice man was killed because they underestimated their intelligence.

DEMON BEAST

The demon beast was the most ferocious of all the animals it encountered. Although, not as smart and cunning as the tubres, it mad up for this in size and brute strength. Only rarely did a group of tubres kill one, using their extra ability of communication.

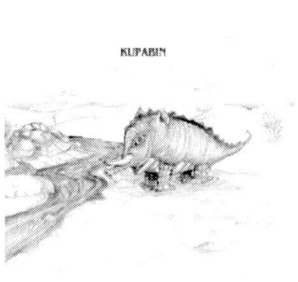

KUPABIN were small defenseless animals. They were great for an easy meal. They survives in great numbers because they were small and could slip into small crevices of cliffs and in small holes in the ice shield. They lived on the abundant crop of ice varmints and lichen, growing on rocks.

APPENDIX C: FACTS ABOUT ANIMALS & BIRDS

BIBUTSAKUFASCORCHUM The Age of Icemen called this beast, bibutsakufascorchum. In their language it meant two headed fire burner. He was so large, dangerous, and powerful that no living creature, who challenged him, lived to talk about it. Literally for centuries he ruled supreme in his kingdom. That was until he ran across the Age of Icemen. With their extra abilities, that they had just acquired from the glowing ball, they were not only able to out smart him, but overpower the beast as well.

DAGGAR was the other fire dragon who thought it was time for another dragon to take over the kingdom. He came into Bibutsakuf's kingdom and challenged him. Daggar was bigger and mightier but with two fire heads and a reputation to maintain, Daggar did not have a chance against Bibutsakuf. Although, he scorched Bibutsakuf's one head, he was not fast enough to finish Bibutsakuf off and the results was of course his own death. The Age of Icemen had Daggar to thank for with a wounded head, for this gave them an advantage over Bibutsakuf which they used to kill him.

RUBALANGERS were insects similar to the bloodsucker but larger and more vicious. They were 6 to 8 inches long and had claws and sharp teeth. Their tongue had a suction tube for the blood.

APPENDIX C: FACTS ABOUT ANIMALS & BIRDS

ARMAFLORVIA

This bird was a huge, nasty bird left over from dinosaur era. It was four to six feet in length and had grasping claws on its middle and end wing. Its beak was long and sharp like that of a raven and razor sharp teeth. On its breast it had armor so that its enemies could not penetrate its body from below. In the contest of wills between the bird and the men, the smartness and the quick action of the Age of Icemen won out.

GOULA

The colony found many new and different animals on their journey and in their new land. One such animal was the goula. The first encounter with the hunters and the goula was when Celestra was giving birth. The hunters had more time to venture out into the forests and mountains to search for their prey. They found many of these goula which looked somewhat like out mountain goats. They also were thrilled by the taste of its meat.

BORGAMUTH

The Age of icemen were surprised to see to shiny eyes in their newly discovered at the Cave of the Three Canyons. It was no animal just one man would want to tackle alone. It was small and vicious, much like our wolverine.

APPENDIX D : FACTS ABOUT THINGS

THE GLOWING BALL OF KNOWLEDGE

After Dimensia 4 broke away from Earth, the Age of Ice people who survived, remained pretty much the same over thousands of years. Theasium took notice and was not satisfied that they hadn't advanced in their culture like others in his galaxy. He gave an assignment to the Order of the High Council of Wizards. They in turned found the solution in designing a Glowing Ball of Knowledge that incorporated advanced thoughts, knowledge, and ideas. When a person touched the ball, it would transfer these into the person in levels they could sustain. The more times a person touched it the further advanced he would be.

The Council appointed Do-o-magnicent to plant the ball where the Age of Icemen could find it. He directed Ohnik to the proper cave gradually most of the leaders and their sons were exposed to the ball. These encounters led to the forming of a colony that traveled to the new and pleasant Promised Land. Trolldar was known throughout many of the galaxies as Wizard of the Mountain Trails and so they appointed him to watch over and guide the colony on their journey from Feriandimal to the Promised Land. When Do-o-magnicent turned evil and became known as Doomagnon, Trolldar became the vigilant keeper of the Glowing Ball of Knowledge as well.

APPENDIX D: FACTS ABOUT THINGS

WORDS, SAYINGS, & HAPPENINGS

Outta Guest who	stranger, visitor, or someone looks different;
Muga Puh	A feeling of disgust;
Hig Pu Hig Pu	kill the enemy;
Upah Wishuga	expression of success;
Butah Mongo	expression of acceptance
Prey	pellget;
Poh Pohs	young punk;
Oh Way Gupah	expression of concern or doubt;
Mura	many;
Feastavor	dining hall;
Feast-till-full	dinner meal;
Feast-a-little	lunch or snack;
Feast-a-early	breakfast;
Magno force	strange phenomena Where sharp magnetic rocks fly back and forth at timed intervals;
Geo-stellar force field	natural phenomena of deep fiery holes in the ground where, at timed intervals, fiery lava and half molten rocks spurt high into the air and return;

APPENDIX D: FACTS ABOUT THINGS

OBJECTS & THINGS

Trees	grostik;
Forests	mura grostik
Bush	bukastiks;
Fruit	plumefrus;
Nuts	cruntebred;
Orchards	mura grostik blumes;
Plantations	mura mukfeas;
Food	feas;
Flowers	blumen;
Muckabok	Herbal mud used by Soothsay to heal.
Toogogood	Herb found on trail with high carbs. It was like half mushroom and half bread.
Umpaga	A root that resembled cattails. Ohnik and Jealon introduced it to the young hunters.
Curastiks	Meat cut into strips, salted, cured & dried to be eaten later.
Sprunga	A weapon invented by Straitona. Resembled a hunting bow.
Swishstiks	Arrow like sticks that Straitona invented to use in his sprunga.

FUTURE COMMUNICATION & ORDERS

IMAGE CONCEPTS
BY HOWARD R VOLLMER

**3915 N Lancaster Circle
Florence, AZ 85132**

Phone: 520 868 ~~3537~~ 8198
E-Mail: hofmiler@cgmailbox.com

Howard R Vollmer